How come she had to be so...fascinating?

Steven reluctantly admitted what he had refused to allow himself to think thus far. In another lifetime, he would have wanted to pursue her and take a good long taste of those lips. As it was...

He wanted her out of his life completely, to hell with those vulnerable blue eyes. He had thought Jackie was most likely a woman who wasn't interested in children. But the way she'd looked when she'd said the word *baby*...

How could he have thought anything would be easy with a woman like that?

But what he wanted right now was to get himself out of this tangled mess. He needed to stop thinking about how she looked and start thinking about how to get her to sign away any rights she had to him and his child.

Ch

Dear Reader,

In this month of tricks or treats, there's no magic to delivering must-read love stories each month. We simply publish upbeat stories from the heart and hope you find them a treat.

What can you do to keep these great stories coming? Plenty! You can write me or visit our online community at www.eHarlequin.com and let me know the stories you like best. Or if you have trouble finding the latest Silhouette Romance titles, be sure to remind your local bookseller how much you enjoy them. This way you will never miss your favorites.

For example, IN A FAIRY TALE WORLD... combines classic love stories, a matchmaking princess and a sprinkling of fairy-tale magic for all-out fun! Myrna Mackenzie launches this Silhouette Romance six-book series with *Their Little Cowgirl* (#1738)—the story of a cowboy and urban Cinderella who lock horns and then hearts over his darling baby daughter.

In *Georgia Gets Her Groom!* (#1739), the latest in Carolyn Zane's THE BRUBAKER BRIDES series, Georgia discovers that Mr. Wrong might be the right man for her, after all. Then watch what happens when a waitress learns her new ranch hand is a tycoon in disguise, in *The Billionaire's Wedding Masquerade* (#1740) by Melissa McClone. And if you like feisty heroines and the wealthy heroes that sweep them off their feet, you'll want to read *Cinderella's Lucky Ticket* by Melissa James (#1741).

Read these romance treats and share the love and laughter with Silhouette Romance this month!

Mavis C. Allen
Associate Senior Editor, Silhouette Romance

Please address questions and book requests to:
Silhouette Reader Service
U.S.: 3010 Walden Ave., P.O. Box 1325, Buffalo, NY 14269
Canadian: P.O. Box 609, Fort Erie, Ont. L2A 5X3

Myrna Mackenzie

THEIR LITTLE COWGIRL

In a Fairy Tale World

SILHOUETTE *Romance*®

Published by Silhouette Books

America's Publisher of Contemporary Romance

Special thanks and acknowledgment are given to
Myrna Mackenzie for her contribution to
the IN A FAIRY TALE WORLD… series.

To my mother, a living example of what a strong heroine
should be. Thanks for always being there for me, Mom.

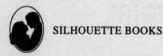 SILHOUETTE BOOKS

ISBN 0-373-19738-1

THEIR LITTLE COWGIRL

MYRNA MACKENZIE,

is the winner of the Holt Medallion honoring outstanding fiction, and was a finalist for numerous other awards, including the Orange Rose, the National Reader's Choice, the *Romantic Times* Reviewer's Choice and WisRWA's Write Touch. She believes that humor, love and hope are three of the best medicines in the world and tries to make sure that her books reflect that belief. Born in a small town in southern Missouri, Myrna grew up in the Chicago area, married her high school sweetheart and has two teenage sons. Her hobbies include dreaming of warmer climes during the cold northern winters, pretending the dust in her house doesn't exist, taking long walks and traveling. Readers can write to Myrna at P.O. Box 225, LaGrange, IL 60525, or they may visit her online at www.myrnamackenzie.com.

The Tale of The Ugly Duckling

When Mother Duck saw the sixth egg in her nest was oddly shaped, she knew one of her children would be different from the rest. Sure enough, that summer, when the ducklings hatched, one was bigger and uglier than the others.

After being kicked aside by his siblings, the ugly one ran away from the pond. But after not much time away, he missed the water and yearned for his true home. As autumn covered the countryside, he headed out into the wide world.

One day, on his journey back to the water, he heard the sound of great flapping wings. In the air, he saw a flock of birds flying high. They were as bright as snow and their long necks were stretched southward. He dreamed of going with them, though he knew he was no fit companion for such beautiful birds.

After a hard, cold winter and plenty of adventures the duckling again saw the flock of beautiful creatures. With his heart in his throat, he decided to follow them. He would risk rejection rather than pass up the chance to take flight with the heavenly beings.

To his surprise, they welcomed him! And when he looked for his dull, awkward reflection in the water, he saw a beautiful swan instead.

Prologue

Merry Montrose, known in another life as Princess Meredith Bessart of Silestia, put her hand on the small of her back and rubbed. She was the manager of La Torchére, an island resort in southwestern Florida, and in early May the island should have been paradise. Many people would have deemed themselves lucky to be here, and she knew that, but Merry just felt rather used up and slightly panicky. She frowned at her companion, Lissa Bessart Piers, the resort's concierge.

"If you had to put a curse on me," Merry told Lissa, "did you have to make me a crone? I think I'm starting to creak."

Lissa smiled slightly. "As your godmother, I have a duty to make sure you either turn out to be a good princess for the people back in your homeland, or that you end up being no princess at all. There was a reason for the curse, as well you know, and there's a way out, as you also know."

Merry wrinkled her nose. "I didn't even do that much. I don't deserve to look and feel so old."

Lissa didn't react.

"All right, maybe I *did* insult Prince Alec a little."

"He was your betrothed and you did more than insult him *a little*. And that wasn't the only thing you did, either."

Merry shrugged. "I suppose you mean that teensy little incident where I tried to break up my father's engagement. It wasn't that big a deal."

"It was a very big deal. He's a king."

"She was older than my father."

"She was his choice, and you not only tried to sabotage the engagement, you took it a step further when that didn't work and did your best to interfere with the wedding itself. You were out of control. Those were hardly the acts of a princess."

"I'm not sorry."

"Even though you're getting older and grayer every day?"

Merry touched her wrinkled face. "All right, I'm a little sorry, and this way out you've discussed, I'm—" She covered her face completely with her hands. "I'm just not sure I'm going to make the deadline. If I don't…"

"You'll always be a crone. Silestia and your ties to your family will be a thing of the past."

"But there's so little time left, and the task is so great. To get twenty-one couples to fall in love and marry, it's almost impossible."

"You only have five to go."

"Yes, but less than a year to do it in."

"You wasted a lot of time when I first put the curse on you. I gave you seven years, all the way to your thirtieth birthday, and the first couple of years you didn't do a thing."

"I know," Merry admitted, surprising herself. "And once I began, it was so difficult. It took me four years and several mismatches to get things straight. I've been doing this long enough now to be realistic. One year is not enough time to ensure that five couples will meet, fall in love and marry. Could you—"

"What?" Lissa asked, her eyes kind, but her voice firm.

"Give me a little more time."

Lissa shook her head sadly. "A princess wouldn't ask for more time."

"So, it's hopeless."

"If you just stand around talking, yes, it is."

Merry let out a sigh. She looked down at herself, at her once beautiful body, now ravaged by age and riddled with aches that even the warm winds of this Florida island couldn't take away. To be like this forever, to never go back to her lovely pampered life…

"All right, I'm working on it," she said. "I just have to keep taking it a step at a time, a couple at a time. Let's look at who's due at the resort this week." She sat down at her computer and called up the schedule of guests. A groan escaped her. Lissa looked over her shoulder.

"I see what you mean," Lissa said. "There doesn't appear to be anyone very promising in this batch. You might have to wait until next week."

But by next week she would be that much closer to losing her youth and beauty and life of royalty forever.

"No, if there aren't two people in this group who are likely to fall in love, well then, I'll just have to choose two people who are unlikely to fall in love and work a little magic."

"Your magic is limited, you know."

"I know." Of course, she knew. She had discovered that time and time again. But all she had was her subtle magic. And, oh yes, she did have one thing more.

"If they won't fit, I'll make them fit," she said defiantly. "I may not have much, but I have determination."

She ran her finger down the list. "There. Him. And her. She's already here, which might make it easier for me to persuade her. And as it happens, the two of them already have a connection of sorts."

Lissa crossed her arms. "It's not a positive connection. They're likely to be adversaries, not lovers."

Merry crossed her arms in kind and glared at her godmother. "You set me a task. I'm tending to that task. You may want me to fail, but I don't intend to do that if I can help it. Now, if you don't mind, I have business to see to. If I'm going to attempt the nearly impossible, I have to rest up. There's matchmaking to be done, whether the man and woman want to be matched or not."

She took a deep breath and stalked off.

Behind her, Lissa smiled. "Oh, I don't want you to fail, my dear. I very much hope you succeed, but, you're right—this is a difficult task. And you've chosen to make it more difficult by trying to match two people who won't appreciate your efforts. For the first time, even I am beginning to doubt that you might make it." And she sighed and went back to work.

Chapter One

"Darn it!" Jacqueline Hammond said to the four walls that surrounded her. She was here in this lovely resort on this lush island to do business, but business wasn't going well at all right now. And Parris, her half sister and business partner, was nowhere to be found.

"I'm not sure we're going to make it," she muttered out loud to herself. "And if we don't make it, we're going to lose the business before we've even gotten started. And then that man, our father, is going to win. He's going to say that we can't do anything right." Which was exactly what he had been thinking ever since Jackie had been born.

And for today, that just might prove to be the truth. Nothing had gone right all morning.

"Well, at least not much more could go wrong," Jackie reasoned out loud.

The telephone on the desk in the temporary office that the resort had provided rang loudly. Jackie groaned. She picked up the receiver.

"Hammond Events," she said, amazed that her voice sounded cool and calm even though she was mentally preparing herself for more bad news.

"Jackie?" The now familiar voice of Merry Montrose, resort manager, flowed crisply through the lines.

"Yes, this is she."

"I'm at the front desk with someone who wants to see you. A rather…interesting someone. I just wanted to let you know that I'll be escorting him to your office."

Ugh, not another celebrity coming to reclaim some family heirloom that yet another family member had tried to sneak into the auction Hammond Events was organizing. Didn't people just donate things out of the goodness of their hearts anymore? Didn't donated items stay donated anymore?

"All right, thank you, Ms. Montrose," Jackie said, trying to keep the weariness and frustration from her voice. It was getting more and more difficult to smile the longer the preparations for the auction went on.

She looked around the room at the collection of items that were starting to stack up. Which precious item was this person going to want to take back? She was beginning to wonder how well any of the donors actually knew the woman who had commissioned Hammond Events to run the auction. Victoria Catherine Smith seemed to have money and the ability to preen with the best of them, but she didn't appear to have any true friends, not when everyone was taking back their stuff.

For a minute, Jackie regretted taking this project on, but then she remembered what was at stake—this business, the only thing that had ever been close to belonging to her, even if she had to share it with a half sister she didn't know very well. If this auction failed, so would the business. There had been no question that they would take on Ms. Smith's auction to raise money to build the Victoria Catherine Memorial Aquarium, slated to showcase some of the local marine life but mostly, Jackie guessed, to showcase Ms. Smith's name to the wealthy who flocked to La Torchére.

The problems with the reluctant donors made it a difficult task, and no doubt it was going to get more difficult within the next few minutes when the unknown man finally made it to her office. She wondered if he was the owner of the Pollock hanging on the wall. She hoped not. It was one of the items most likely to draw crowds to the auction. She frowned at the painting.

"It doesn't look that bad to me," a male voice said.

Jackie whirled and found herself staring up into the face of a tall, dark-haired, broad-shouldered man. His face was tanned, his eyes nearly black and unreadable. And though he'd seemed to be making a joke, there was no trace of levity in his expression. Indeed, the way he was studying her made him look a bit like a hunter, and she felt more than a bit like his prey.

With great effort, she forced herself to smile and ignore that ridiculous thought.

"Is it yours?" she asked.

He blinked. No, it obviously wasn't. "It's hanging in your office," he pointed out.

"Yes, but it's an item for the auction I'm hosting and…well, never mind. How can I help you, Mr…."

"Rollins. Steven Rollins."

His voice was deep, the words rolling off his tongue in a soft, sexy drawl. Jackie couldn't help noticing that he seemed too big and masculine for the room. Even so, he looked very much in control, as if this was his office rather than hers.

The thought made her angry. She had been forced to share almost everything of importance all of her life.

Jackie frowned, then realized how silly she was being. This was business. She had to be nice. "How can I help you, Mr. Rollins? Are you here about the auction, or is there some other business you would like Hammond Events to handle?"

He stared directly at her—those dark, compelling eyes seeming to gaze into places no man had ever looked before. "I don't want to buy anything from you, Ms. Hammond, and I certainly don't want to sell you anything that belongs to me."

He said this last part with just a bit too much emphasis.

Jackie blinked and took a deep breath for courage. "Perhaps you should just tell me what you *do* want, Mr. Rollins."

"Perhaps I should, but I think you might want to be sitting down when I tell you what I want with you." His voice dropped lower, and for a minute Jackie felt slightly disoriented. To her surprise, Steven Rollins walked behind her desk and pulled out her chair. He nodded to her and, like an obedient puppy, she slipped around behind the desk and sat. He still stood behind her.

She started to turn the chair, but he circled it and leaned against her desk beside her. A seemingly casual pose, but there was nothing casual about this man.

Jackie felt her breath catch. She had always been a quiet person, and until she had taken on this business with Parris she had considered herself a behind-the-scenes kind of woman. It had taken a lot of work and practice and effort to teach herself how to appear bold and outgoing when inside she was often shaking. It was quite a task to hide her nervousness and make people feel at ease, but she had learned to push past her anxieties and concentrate on the customer and the task. Now this man was making her forget all her hard-won lessons. More to the point, he was making her aware of herself as a woman, which was totally unacceptable.

"What do you want from me, Mr. Rollins?" she asked.

He stared into her eyes and then shook his head. "Ms. Hammond, I regret to tell you that we have a problem, a big one, and it doesn't involve paintings or auctions, either. The fact is that it has just come to my attention that you are the mother of my baby," he said. "We need to do something about that."

Jackie's eyes widened. Her breathing stopped. She slipped one hand over her throat.

"What?" she finally managed in a whisper.

He shrugged and rubbed the back of his neck. "I probably should have led up to that a bit more slowly, but…you donated eggs at one time?"

Her eyes widened. She gripped the arms of her chair as if squeezing something hard could turn back time. "Yes, once, but only to my cousin," she said weakly. Her cousin, Trish, had given birth to a girl, and Jackie's four-year-old niece, Chloe, was a sweetheart. And she was the *only* result of Jackie's donation. "You're not trying to tell me that you and Trish...I wouldn't believe that, no matter how good looking you are. She's madly in love with her husband."

The man's left brow had raised slightly when she told him he was good looking. "Never had the honor of meeting the lady," was all he said. "And it was my late wife who gave birth to my little girl."

Jackie felt suddenly sick. "I don't understand."

"That makes two of us, Ms. Hammond."

"There must be some mistake."

"There was. Apparently your donor eggs were implanted in my wife without your permission. I'm terribly sorry about that."

A baby. There was another baby with her DNA, another child she would never get to hold as her own. Chloe had been one thing, she had been voluntary, but this...

Jackie pushed her chin up, her hair falling back as she gazed up at the man with the unreadable eyes. "Why should I believe you, Mr. Rollins?"

"Why should I lie to you?"

"I don't know, but I...there might be a reason that hasn't occurred to me yet."

"I assure you that I'm telling the truth, even though I wish it weren't so. I do, of course, have proof."

He reached into the pocket of his navy sport coat,

the movement making the muscles bunch beneath his white shirt.

Jackie blanched. How could she even notice such a thing at a moment like this? She turned her attention to the paper Steven Rollins was holding out.

"What is that?" Her voice was barely a whisper.

"It's the paperwork showing which eggs were used to bring about my wife's pregnancy. And this other paper matches those very eggs to you."

Jackie's hand shook as she took the crisp white pieces of paper. She read the words, which blurred before her eyes.

"How could this have happened?" she asked herself out loud.

"I've asked myself that, but there just aren't any good answers."

Biting her lip, Jackie nodded and dared to glance up into the dark eyes of the tall man beside her. He didn't look happy.

"It's very…very generous of you to come to me with this news. You didn't have to. I would never have known."

"Possibly."

She could tell by his expression that he had considered not coming to her.

"Why *did* you come?"

"Believe me, my reasons for being here today are anything but altruistic, Ms. Hammond. Suzy isn't a lost puppy that I was willing to return to the original owners if they showed up when I placed a sign in a store window. I would have liked nothing better than to leave you in the dark. But other people knew. At least a few at the hospital did. These kinds of things have a way of leaking out."

"So here you are."

"Yes." The word seemed to have been forced out of him. He leveled a long, dark stare at her. She noticed that his jaw was hard and square, the skin taut over the bone. He had the look of a man's man about him, the kind of man many women would have paid to have stare at them. But she wasn't like most women, and being studied this closely by Steven Rollins made her breath kick up hard in her chest. Her heart was doing sprints. She wanted to squirm.

"What exactly do you want from me, Mr. Rollins?" She managed to keep her voice reasonably firm, even though she knew her knuckles were clenched on the chair so hard that they were undoubtedly white.

He pushed off the desk and rose to his feet, intimidatingly tall. "I want your name on a different piece of paper, Ms. Hammond, stating that you relinquish all rights to my daughter," he said quietly, in a voice that brooked no arguments. "And I want your word that you will never try to see her or contact her. And you, in return, will have my word and my name on a legal document stating that I will never darken your door again. That's why I'm here. That's exactly what I want from you. Now, do we have a deal, ma'am?"

Jackie had never been a person who argued. She had spent her life being accommodating. She had spent her girlhood trying to please a man who could not be pleased and jumping to do his will in the rare moments when he even noticed her. She had never had anything or anyone who truly belonged to her in any real sense. So yes, she had donated her eggs to Trish and been happy to do so. Chloe was worth the hurt of knowing she could never call the little girl her own. But now here was this man, trying to stare her down, trying to force her yet again to give in and be good, to do the easy thing as she had always done.

Somewhere there was a child, a baby, who through accident had come from *her* body, Jackie thought. A child she would never even have the chance to see the way she saw Chloe.

She stared up at Steven Rollins.

"You think you have the right to do this."

For a moment his eyelids flickered. Then it was as if his whole body turned to steel. "I *know* I have the right. Suzy is mine. You didn't even know about her. I didn't have to come here."

Jackie studied the rigid line of his jaw. "But you would have had to live with the fear that someday I might find out."

"Yes." He bit the word off, and she understood that it was hard for him to admit as much to her. It was obvious that his child meant a great deal to him.

"How old?"

"What?" A muscle twitched in his jaw. He shook his head.

"How old is…is Suzy?"

He hesitated, as if even sharing that much was too much. "She's one."

"A baby. Still a baby." With all the things that came

with a baby—smiles and giggles and soft skin and a baby powder scent. Unconditional love and acceptance of those who cared for her. Sweetness. Innocence. A child who wouldn't exist if not for those eggs she had donated. A part of herself. Jackie almost closed her eyes, the longing was so overwhelming.

"You'll sign?" Steven Rollins's strong voice broke into her thoughts and she looked at him. For a moment she thought she saw a flash of fear and pain in his eyes.

He had lived with his baby for a whole year. She was precious to him. She was, in fact, his and his alone. Suzy Rollins was out of reach for the woman who had unwittingly helped to give her life. Suzy would never know Jackie, and that was the way it had to be.

An unexpected pain sliced through Jackie. She knew she had to sign the papers. And she would.

"Have you come far? Where do you live?"

"I don't see how that has anything to do with anything."

"Please." Her voice caught, and she hated that sign of weakness. She'd spent so much time learning to disguise her weaknesses.

But Steven Rollins seemed to soften at her tone. "I live on a ranch. Around Claxton."

"Not that far."

"No."

A tiny hope filled Jackie's soul. "I understand why you want me to sign, Mr. Rollins. I would do the same." To have to share a loved one could be horrible and very difficult. "I don't expect you to share your daughter with a stranger, especially one who didn't even know of her existence before today."

The man relaxed even more. A small smile turned his face heartbreakingly handsome, making Jackie's breathing kick up a notch. No doubt he'd had a beautiful wife.

"Thank you, Ms. Hammond. You'll sign then?" He held out his hand, a conciliatory gesture.

"Yes, but I have a condition."

Immediately his hand stilled. He pulled back. "What kind of a condition?"

"I want to meet her."

"What do you mean, you want to meet her?"

His tone was thunderous. Jackie should have been shaking in her shoes. Under other circumstances, she would have been, but for some reason she wasn't as scared of Steven Rollins as she should have been. Maybe because he seemed to genuinely care for his daughter.

And the truth was that she wasn't completely sure what she had meant by her words. She just knew that she did mean them. She had given up one child, and it had been much more difficult than she could ever have believed possible. Never once had she gotten to hold that baby as if it were her own. But fate and happenstance had combined to give her one more chance.

Jackie wanted that chance desperately.

"I meant what I said, Mr. Rollins. You just told me that your daughter was conceived from eggs that came from my body. There's a part of me in her. That's something I don't take lightly. I'm not asking to be a lasting part of her life, you understand. I know there's no possibility of that, but I…I just can't sign a paper and never once have a glimpse of her. I want the chance to see her."

"Impossible. You can't do it."

Oh, she had heard those words so many times in her life. And she had often believed them.

But this time a child was involved.

"I can do it, Mr. Rollins."

He studied her carefully, slowly, maddeningly. Jackie almost held her breath as his gaze drifted over her, as if looking for flaws, missing nothing. She felt suddenly awkward and naked in her boxy gray suit. In that moment he was a man looking over a woman. And she was a woman reacting in the most physical way, her body and skin prickling with heightened awareness, Jackie was horrified to realize. No doubt the man was merely trying to intimidate her. And so, with great difficulty, she managed to sidestep her body's reaction.

"We'll see about your demands," he finally said. "I'll talk to you tomorrow."

Jackie was pretty sure that he was going to come back armed with plenty of legal advice. And he would look her over again.

The legal advice didn't scare her...too much. The look—she didn't want to think about that look—was too intimate.

"I'll let you know my terms then," she agreed. "I'll have them in writing."

He gave her a curt nod. She almost missed the look that lurked in the back of his eyes, but just before he turned, she saw it. Fear?

She held out her hand to his retreating back. She should just leave it alone.

"Mr. Rollins?"

He turned on one heel.

"I'm assuming it will take a certain amount of money to make you go away," he told her with an unmistakable trace of derision.

Slowly she shook her head. "I'm not interested in money. And I don't mean to be difficult, but I can't just leave this alone. We're talking about a child. A baby."

"I know," he said. His voice was tight, the emotion leashed, but not completely.

That got to her—the fact that he was trying to hide how badly he cared about his child, but couldn't. The fact that he could affect her that way made him dangerous.

She wished she never had to see him again.

"I'll see you tomorrow," she said.

Chapter Two

"**D**amn woman," Steven bit off the words as he pulled off his boots and dropped them on the opulent cream-colored carpeting of the room he had booked at La Torchére. What was her game? Why was she pushing this issue when she had only just discovered Suzy's existence?

And how come she had to be so...so...

"Fascinating." He reluctantly admitted what he had refused to allow himself to think thus far. Jacqueline Hammond was no beauty by a long shot. In truth, she was rather plain, but she had a pair of fine blue eyes and pretty pink lips that trembled ever so slightly at moments of high emotion. In another lifetime, had he been another man, he would have wanted to pursue her and take a good long taste of those lips. As it was...

"I want her out of my life completely. To hell with those vulnerable blue eyes." He pounded out the words.

He meant them, too. It was going to be hard raising Suzy alone, especially once she reached an age when she needed the kinds of things that a woman could best provide. But he was through with relationships and especially with marriage and dreams. Too many of his dreams had been wrenched away from him.

All he wanted right now was to get himself out of this tangled mess with Jacqueline Hammond and get back to his daughter and his ranch. Then everything would be fine.

He had thought this would be easy. He had assumed Jacqueline Hammond was most likely a woman who had once done a good deed but wasn't interested in children herself.

But that look in her eyes when she'd said the word baby…

"Dammit all!" How could he have thought anything would be easy with a woman like that?

What he needed right now was to stop thinking about how she had looked and start thinking about how to get her to sign away any rights she had to him and his child.

He picked up the phone and began to dial.

The next morning, Jackie entered the forest-green, cream and golden oak lobby of La Torchére with both dread and anticipation. She had gone upstairs last night still reeling from the shock of the news that she had helped produce a child, and still shaking from her encounter with Steven Rollins. She had had few close relationships with men over the years, and had never had a good one. She no longer even wanted to try, so coming into close contact with a man who sent her senses spinning out of control and who, of all men, had reason to dislike her, was more than disconcerting.

She really didn't want to see him again. But there was no way she was giving up this opportunity.

Jackie wondered what Steven Rollins would think of the simple plan she had formulated in the wee hours of the night as she lay tossing and turning.

Whatever he thought, it wouldn't be something positive. Ducking into a deserted alcove, she pulled out a small mirror from her purse to make sure she looked composed. She did. Her dark hair was in place, her eyes gave nothing away.

A changeling child, her blond gorgeous mother had once called Jackie with disgust. Plain, nondescript, unnoticeable, her looks had simply emphasized how she had never fit in. But today she hoped that her unremarkable, restrained exterior would stand her in good stead. She needed to be firm, to appear unshakeable.

She would be, Jackie decided, and satisfied that she had managed to erase her emotions from her expression, she took a deep breath and headed for her office to wait for another disturbing encounter.

This time she would not let him get to her. She wouldn't even think of him as a man, but only as the doorway to an opportunity to make a few memories with a sweet little child.

"Jackie." Merry's imperious voice stopped Jackie in her tracks. She turned and looked at the elegant but fading woman.

"Did you need me, Merry?"

"Not exactly, but you might need me if you're looking for Mr. Rollins. I've set him and his papers up at a shaded table in view of the beach. I thought the atmosphere might make your business more pleasant." The woman tried a smile, but it was clear that she wasn't usually the cheerful type. That was okay. Merry had been more than accommodating to Hammond Events. Perhaps too accommodating, Jackie suddenly thought.

The last thing she wanted was to sit with Steven Rollins in a secluded, romantic setting. But she wanted to get this over with quickly, to get past it so she could see the baby she had helped bring into the world.

"Thank you, Merry." She nodded.

Merry tilted her head. "I'll lead you to him."

There was nothing to do but follow and hope that she could retain her cool and calm.

But when Jackie came to the end of the path, she nearly balked when she realized that Merry had led her to one of the bowers at the edge of the beach. Surrounded by palm trees, exotic foliage and blossoms, the bower enclosed a small shelter complete with a linen-covered table for two and a convenient double hammock. The scent of flowers drifted in, setting the stage for those who were looking for romance. A waiter appeared with a golden tray of cold drinks in sparkling crystal.

Jackie blinked.

"A person can't conduct business on a hot day without something to slake her thirst can she?" Merry mused as the waiter approached the table.

But Jackie had moved on to other thoughts. Steven

Rollins had risen to his feet at their approach. He nod-ded to the waiter and to Merry, who withdrew. He was wearing an open-necked white shirt tucked into jeans that molded to his thighs. His sleeves were rolled up, re-vealing strong tanned arms.

"Ms. Hammond," he said with a slight nod of his head as he held out his hand.

She hesitated, noting that his fingers were long and brown, his palm callused. He was a rancher, wasn't he? And though he had every reason to hate her his man-ners would never show that.

Old fashioned, she thought, and then she resisted the urge to close her eyes as she slid her hand into his, feel-ing the warmth and strength of his grip for one short sec-ond before he released her.

"Mr. Rollins." She sat, and he followed suit.

"I was wondering if you were going to actually go through with this," he began.

"Hoping I wouldn't, I think you mean," she countered.

He shrugged and kept his direct gaze on her. "I'd like to keep this simple."

A small bit of hope crept in. "Then we agree on something. I want to keep things as simple and easy as possible, too."

"You said you wanted to meet my daughter. I won't pretend to like that, but I've decided that I'll agree to it. I suppose I can bring her here next week, arrange for a few hours together."

His tone was uncompromising, though his voice wasn't nearly as harsh as it had been yesterday.

She wondered what he would say to her suggestion.

He wouldn't like it. She knew that much, just as she knew that she might lose her courage if she didn't just plunge in.

"I want two weeks," she said, her voice breaking only slightly.

The long silence that followed was heavy, laced with unmistakable anger. Steven Rollins's eyes were like dark smoldering flames.

"No. You've got to be kidding."

"I don't, generally. I—"

He held up one hand. "I'm not even going to discuss this. This is *my* daughter you're talking about."

"I know that." And this time her voice wasn't calm or cool or any of the things she wanted it to be. "I know that," she said again, trying to bring the emotion down a notch. "And I understand what you're thinking. You want me to sign away my right to Suzy forever and you want me to do it now. Well, I'm prepared to do that. I'll sign this very minute. I'll agree to disappear completely when we're done, but first I want the right to spend just a short time with her. Two weeks is such a small amount of time, and it's all I'm asking for. I have the right to ask, you know."

"I could fight you in court."

"You could, but someone would have to explain how those eggs ended up in the wrong place. That could take lots of time. This could drag out. You give me my two weeks, and I'm gone for good. It's over, and you and Suzy can get on with your lives without me."

He scrubbed one hand back through his dark hair. "Why are you doing this? You didn't even know she existed before yesterday. She can't mean anything to you."

And she obviously meant everything to this man. Jackie knew that. She honored it, but...

She took a moment to gather her thoughts. She raised her chin, her hair falling back as she gazed way up into Steven's eyes. "I'm doing this because I gave up a child once before. I freely donated the eggs that time, and there was no question of me ever having time alone with the baby when she was born. I didn't think it would matter, but it did. Giving a child life, and her mother hope, has been one of the most wonderful experiences of my life, but also one of the most painful. Chloe can never know about me, at least not until she's much older. Her mother, Trish, and I are cousins, and it would only complicate things to tell her child that I'm her biological mother. I know that, and I accept it. I chose it, so I don't have a problem with the situation.

"But this time is different. My eggs were used without my permission, and I'm incensed about that. Somewhere on your ranch is a little girl who started out as a part of me, however much you dislike that fact. This time I get the chance to do things differently. I get the chance to be a part, however small, of her life. And it can work because she's young enough that she'll never remember me. *You'll* never remember much of me, but I'll have something to hold in my heart forever. I'll walk away, Mr. Rollins. You'll have my word and my legal, unbreakable signature before witnesses as a guarantee. Just don't ask me to sign Suzy away without ever having seen her. Don't be that cruel. Would you simply walk away if someone had told you that she was out there and that you had fathered her?"

Steven opened his mouth to speak, but then he closed it again. "Is this how you get people to donate expensive artwork to your auctions, Ms. Hammond? By blackmailing them?"

Heat and anger rolled through Jackie, but she subdued them. The man was testing her, and she wouldn't be tested. She'd jumped through hoops for her father, and later for Garret, a man who had claimed to love her for a time. She'd given up her own wishes too many times and all to no avail. "You came to me, not the other way around," she reminded the man.

As the seconds ticked by they stared at each other, a silent standoff. Then he held out his hands, palms out.

"You're a hard woman, Ms. Hammond."

His comment caught Jackie off guard. She had been called many things in her lifetime—invisible, shy, maternal, sweet, a marshmallow, a leaf blowing in the wind, a pushover. But then she had never had anyone come to her with this kind of news before. And she had never faced the prospect of giving away her baby without ever having the chance to see her face even once. She rather liked being hard in this instance. This was a situation that called for hard and pushy, and for the first time in her life she was rising to the occasion.

"After we sign the papers, you'll bring Suzy here?" she asked.

"No. Not here. You'll come to my home, and that is something I'm not budging on, Ms. Hammond. I have a ranch, and I'm needed there. I can't just run off for two weeks, and I won't let Suzy go anywhere unless I'm there. My ranch or nothing."

Jackie blanched inside, but she refused to allow herself to think. "All right, your ranch, but we go right away. I'm ready."

Steven gave her a long, lingering once-over—from the tip of her shiny sedate hairstyle, past her pale cream dress, to the bottom of her sensible pumps. She almost thought he was going to smile. "You don't look like you're ready for a ranch," he mused.

She wasn't, not really. The thought of horses and cows and bulls and who knew what else scared her to death. "I'll go wherever your child is," she said firmly. "For two weeks I'll be there and then I'll return here where I belong. I'll vanish like mist in the sunlight, and you won't have to worry about me ever again."

He gave her a short, slow nod. "I'll hold you to that," he said, "and if you ever try to break our bargain, I will come after you with every weapon I possess. Anyone who tries to steal my daughter had better run, and run fast."

But Jackie was pretty sure that no one would ever be able to run fast enough if Steven Rollins wanted to catch them. She had a feeling that she had just bitten off a lot more than she could chew. Steven Rollins was more man than she had ever tackled.

The very thought of tackling or tangling with him was...

"Frightening," she said out loud, later in her room. But in her mind, she heard another word.

Exhilarating.

She had never felt so alive as she had yesterday and today, arguing with this man who clearly wished she would disappear in a puff of blue smoke.

And she had just agreed to go live on a ranch with that same, too-handsome man who hated her. How on earth was she going to survive for the next fourteen days? She'd done all right here in this environment where she felt at home, but what weapons would she possess once she was out of her element and alone with him?

"What do you mean, you're leaving me in charge?" Jackie's sister, Parris, was clearly not happy about Jackie's decision. "You can't just pack up and go off to some ranch and leave me to do all the work."

Jackie tactfully refrained from mentioning that Parris had done very little of the work regarding the company thus far. Not that that was surprising. Parris had never had to work for anything. When Jackie's father had divorced her mother and remarried Parris's mom, Jackie had worked extra hard to secure her father's attention. But it never seemed to make a bit of difference. He didn't want to be with Jackie. He had found another daughter, and his oldest child's efforts didn't matter all that much. And three years ago, when Jackie had imagined herself in love with Garret Brickwater, she had done her best to make the relationship work, but Garret had taken one look at Parris's beauty and had no use for her older sister anymore.

That was just the way it was. Jackie had never fit with anyone. Even her own mother had resented her existence, claiming that having a baby had caused her to lose her figure and thus, her husband. Jackie had always been the outsider, the ugly duckling with no real place to call her own.

She certainly didn't belong on a ranch with Steven Rollins, but she was going anyway. And the truth was that, if she and Parris were ever going to make a go of this company, Parris was going to have to take part in the operation.

"You'll be just fine," Jackie told her sister. "And I'll only be a phone call away."

"Jackie, you're going to a ranch, for heaven's sake, with cows and cow-related things and…and manure. It may only be a phone call away, but it's also the edge of the world. And what if something comes up that's too complicated to handle? What do I do if another someone wants to take back a donation?"

Jackie sighed. "Do your best to be gracious and charming, Parris. Remember that this business is all we have. It's what we live on."

"So why are you leaving? You've never even met that baby."

She had explained the details to Parris already. "I want something this business can't give me," she told her sister.

"What's that?"

"I don't know. I just know I have to do this. And anyway, I'll only be gone two weeks. How wrong can things go in that time?"

She and Parris exchanged a look. Things were going wrong every day. The whole operation could collapse. She really wanted to bring Suzy here.

But somehow she knew that even a court wouldn't insist that Steven rip his child from her home on a forced visit to an egg donor. She wasn't even sure the courts would give her any rights. Obviously this was shaky ground all the way around, or he wouldn't have let her have her way at all. Neither of them wanted to risk the legal system.

"I'll check in all the time," Jackie promised. "If someone is being especially difficult, I'll call them or we'll arrange a conference call or even a video connection. Somehow we'll keep the business alive."

"All right, if there's no other way."

There wasn't. If there was any way she could avoid going to stay in Steven Rollins's home—where he would be around every day watching her every move, making her remember how it had felt to have him touch her hand—she would have jumped at it. But there wasn't.

Somehow she was just going to have to learn how to stay out of the man's way. What she needed was a plan.

"Do you think this will work?" Merry asked Lissa.

"Do I think they're attracted? Of course they are. He's a very masculine man and she's very sweet with lovely eyes. They're attracted, but do I think they'll fall in love?" Lissa frowned.

"You're right. I've thoroughly checked into both of their pasts. Steven was forced to give up his dream of a football career and then his dream of a fulfilling marriage, so now he's through with anything vaguely romantic. And he doesn't want her, or any woman, on his ranch or near his child. As for Jackie, she doesn't want to go near a man, and the ranch thing…"

Merry suddenly looked at her godmother with stricken eyes. "It's not going to work, is it?"

"Well, they hardly seem suited," Lissa began, "and they *are* moving off the resort, where you won't have much control."

"And already days have passed," Merry said. "I've wasted time on them, but I don't have any new prospects at the moment. That's it. I'm just going to have to do my best to work a miracle long-distance." She pulled a cell phone with a screen for color pictures from the pocket of her dress.

"What are you doing, Merry?"

"You know what I'm doing. I'm using what little useful magic I have to watch them." She could use the phone to watch what happened on Steven's ranch. "I'm not sure what I can do when I'll be here and they're on a ranch, but if I see a promising circumstance, then I'll…"

"You'll what?"

"I'll do something. Anything."

"Careful, Merry. You remember the first time you tried to force two people together who didn't fit. Both of them vowed never to get involved with anyone again, and they haven't to this day."

"I know. That was a mistake. I'm not going to make any mistakes with Jackie and Steven—I hope."

Chapter Three

The trip to Rollins Acres wasn't very far, which was a good thing, Steven mused the next day after they had disembarked from the ferry to the mainland. Because if ever two people were less suited to spend time closed up in a truck together it was himself and Jacqueline Hammond. The mere fact that the woman had not balked at riding in a pickup truck was in itself amazing.

She clearly didn't belong here. Dressed in a dove gray suit that hit just above a very pretty pair of knees, her dark hair pulled back in a low, sleek ponytail with a silver clip, she was the epitome of refinement and primness.

"You ever ride in a pickup truck before?" he caught himself asking, a trace of amusement lifting his lips.

She gave him a look that told him she didn't like being laughed at. "Well, I usually only ride in golden pumpkins pulled by white horses," she said, "but don't worry. I can stifle my inner stuffiness long enough to withstand a ride in a pickup truck. And for the record, Mr. Rollins, I wouldn't exactly call this a pickup truck in the conventional sense. You've got a DVD player, a GPS, more cup holders than one man could possibly use and leather seats. If this were a colder climate, I'll bet you would have heaters in the seats, too." She gave him a placid knowing smile.

He couldn't keep from chuckling. "Touché, Ms. Hammond. I probably had that coming, but my point was…"

She sighed. "I know your point, Mr. Rollins. I don't belong on a ranch. For the record, I did buy a pair of jeans, and I'll eventually wear them. I just…it's just…I'll be meeting your daughter for the first time and I…"

Her voice trailed off, and suddenly he realized that she was nervous, genuinely nervous about meeting a baby. This self-assured woman who had dared to stand toe-to-toe with him—a six foot one male with a body grown hard from work—was nervous. She hadn't given an inch, even when he had pushed her and even when it was obvious that he was making her uncomfortable. She'd stood her ground, but now she had dressed to impress a one-year-old child.

"Well, Suzy is pretty partial to gray," he said, turning to give her a smile, hoping to lighten the mood, "but she's going to be mighty disappointed that you're not wearing pearls and white gloves."

To his surprise, she shook her head and smiled back. Not just a weak, polite smile, either, but a brilliant one that made his breathing stop and sent heat sizzling through his body in a powerful flow. "I was thinking maybe the diamond tiara," she quipped.

"Just the thing," he agreed amiably, but inside him a storm was brewing. His sudden reaction to that smile had been a warning for him to stay away from this woman. He was through with anything involving emotional needs of a deep or serious nature. He had lost too much—his football career, nearly his marriage, and then, when he and Michelle had finally put things back together again and he had begun to hope for at least a partially happy ending, he'd lost his wife, too. So, other than an occasional visit to another town and a woman there who, like himself, wanted nothing more than a meaningless physical fling, he kept his distance from women. He hadn't been tempted so far, and it wasn't going to happen now, especially with a woman who could only mean trouble and regret.

"Here we are. This is my ranch, Ms. Hammond," he said, turning in at a gate that declared them to now be on Rollins Acres. "This is where you'll be spending the next two weeks. I think you can safely leave your tiara in the box."

He glanced across and ended up gazing right into those beautiful blue eyes. "Maybe you're right about the tiara," she said softly. "But, do you think you could call me Jackie for the next two weeks? If we're going to be seeing a lot of each other…"

"We won't," he said suddenly and then realized how harsh his voice had been. He had agreed to her terms. Being rude and abrupt would only make this time harder. "I only meant that you'll probably be mostly interested in the house," he explained. "Suzy spends most of her time there. I won't be around that much except in the evenings, but yes, I see your point. I'm not all that used to being called Mr. Rollins, and Steven will be fine."

He continued down the long road leading to the house and glanced to the side again. She looked incredulous.

"What?"

"You'd let me spend time alone with Suzy?" For some reason she seemed a bit indignant.

"That would be a bad thing?"

"She's a baby. I'm a total stranger."

He stopped the car. "You are an enigma, Ms.—Jackie. You force me to take you into my house for two weeks so you can be with my child, and now you're getting huffy because you think I'm not taking enough care with her?"

"I am not huffy." She had her arms crossed under her breasts. He took a long look at what he hadn't noticed before beneath her loose clothing, then glanced up to see that she was blushing. She brought her arms up higher, covering herself. "I'm not huffy," she repeated.

He couldn't help grinning. "You most definitely are, and you're also embarrassed. Relax, Jackie. I don't assault my guests, and no, I don't intend to leave you alone with my daughter. She has a nanny."

"Oh." The sound was hollow and small.

"Yes, oh. No offense, Jackie, but I don't trust anyone I've just met with Suzy. The nanny, Ms. Lerner, had to give me five personal and five professional references and I had a detective check her out. I don't take chances when it comes to my child."

She nodded. "Did you do that with me? Hire a detective, I mean?"

He hadn't, even though he'd had his attorney run a basic check on her background. She had come up completely clean—the eldest daughter of Jeffrey Hammond, a wealthy entrepreneur known for looking out only for himself and the bottom line. Her mother was dead, her only relative other than her mostly absent father was the half sister who was her business partner. No highs, no lows. But glancing at her profile, at the lush curves beneath that mannish suit, Steven wondered if he shouldn't find out more. Surely she'd had a number of men fighting to be the one to bed that body. There could be plenty of skeletons he had missed.

"Is there something you'd like to tell me, Jackie?" he asked. "Some past sin you want to admit to, something that might make you unfit to spend time with my child?"

She gave him a long, assessing stare, then raised one delicate shoulder in a gesture of dismissal. "I once filched a box of Belgian chocolates from my mother's dresser. So yes, I do have some terribly bad, incurable habits and a criminal history. If you don't watch out, I might turn Suzy into a chocoholic like myself. I *am* a dangerous woman, Steven."

She dared him to say differently. He couldn't. That smile and those eyes, but most of all that hint of the vulnerable, made her very dangerous. She made a man want to kiss her, whether she tasted of stolen chocolates or just woman.

"Then I'll keep my eye on you," he told her. And he

meant it, too. He couldn't be careless with Suzy, even if he wanted to keep his distance from this woman.

He pulled the car up in front of the house, a wide two-story farmhouse with a porch that wrapped around three sides.

"What a pretty shade of pale blue," she said, referring to the color of the clapboards. "Rather a feminine color, though. I wouldn't have expected it of a man who drives a huge, black look-at-me-I'm-all-man truck."

Steven chuckled. "The house color was my wife's choice."

Jackie's eyes grew solemn. "I'm sorry."

"Don't be. You just asked about the paint. Asking questions is not what you need to be sorry about." Okay, he couldn't stop implying that she should have stayed back at the resort.

"I know, but…has it been long since you lost your wife?"

"She died the day Suzy was born, so now it's just my daughter and me. That's all it will ever be, too." He knew the words sounded as though he was warning her away. But they were really meant for himself—a reminder that, while he might be bringing a desirable woman to his home, she was not there for his pleasure.

"I understand. I don't have much interest in men, either."

He raised one brow.

She blushed. "That is, I just don't get along all that well with them, at least not in the long-term. I like answering only to myself, and I don't intend for it to be any other way. I fit myself better than any man could ever fit me."

Ah, so she had barriers, too. She hadn't been involved with a man for awhile and she didn't want one now or ever. That should have made him very happy.

Instead it just made him wonder exactly how long it had been since a man had kissed her until they were both breathless and mindless and aching and when it would happen again.

Jackie was a lot more worried about her reaction to Steven than her reaction to his truck. Trucks couldn't make a woman feel all hot and bothered, at least not a woman like her. But every time Steven glanced her way, she was incredibly conscious of the fact that she was a woman—the kind of thing that pretty much never happened with her.

Not that any of that could be important now. In just a minute, she was going to meet the child who held a part of her. Someone who was at least a little bit like her.

She twisted her fingers together as Steven moved around the truck to help her down. Her hand felt cold in his warm one as he reached up and touched her.

"She's just a baby," he reminded her, and this time his eyes were even a little kind.

"I haven't known any babies really. What if I don't know what to do?"

"Babies have a way of making you forget to think. Just let it happen," he suggested.

At that moment a squeal of tires and flying bits of gravel signaled a new arrival.

"Ben," was all Steven said, but the man was already jumping from his truck, a look of consternation on his face.

"Come on, Steven," the man said. "Sorry to jump you like this, but we have a little problem. Hoagie was messing around doing doughnuts in the field, showing off for the boys, and he's gone and clipped the fence at the south pasture with his new SUV. Now we've got our randiest bulls mixing in with Mrs. Redfern's cows, and you know how she gets about her dainty ladies. When I saw the dust from your tires, I left the boys working to deal with things and came here full tilt."

Steven muttered something beneath his breath, a word Jackie was pretty certain he would never utter around his daughter. He looked at her and then at the house. And then back in the direction that Ben had come. She understood—he didn't want to leave her here with his child while he tended to the emergency.

She probably should be angry, but after her lecture about leaving his child open to strangers, she could hardly be that.

"I'll just wait in the truck," she volunteered.

He didn't stop to argue, just made sure she was in the seat before he shut the door, then hopped back in and raced across the field behind Ben.

"Thank you. I'm sorry."

"Is there any danger?"

"Not really. Just the danger of my bulls taking advantage of Mrs. Redfern's cows. Mrs. Redfern doesn't approve of illicit mating of animals. She doesn't have many cows, but the ones she has are considered pets and they're all artificially inseminated. Not that she can stop nature, but…well, she has a point. My animals don't have any business straying onto her land. It's my concern if that happens. Not a neighborly way to be. If a man can't control his own herd—or in this case, his own men—he doesn't have any business being a rancher."

"But you weren't even here."

"Doesn't matter. I'm in charge. I'm sure you feel that way about your business, too. Even though you're gone, things have to run smoothly."

For half a panicked second, Jackie worried about the fact that she had left Parris at the helm. She saw what Steven meant. But then he was pulling the truck to a sudden stop. There were horses tethered to another vehicle.

"I have to ride from here. Mrs. Redfern is a purist, so I can't bring the vehicle onto her property unless we're on the roads. Don't get out of the truck," Steven told Jackie.

Hot anger lurched through her. "I'm no danger to your ranch," she told the man. "I don't intend to sabotage you just because I don't like you."

He blinked at that. "I wasn't worried about that. I just don't want you getting hurt. Do you have any idea how much a full-grown bull or cow weighs?"

"A lot?"

He shook his head and smiled slightly. "Yes, a lot would be a good guess. And you're a city girl. I don't want you getting a broken foot, or worse. People might think I set you up to get rid of you."

He was still smiling, but she wasn't sure if he was kidding. She chose to think he was. "I'll stay in the truck."

"You do that, city girl."

And then he moved to one of the horses, joining Ben as the two of them rode off.

She was trapped inside a mountain of a truck, surrounded by nothing but grass and a few skimpy trees,
wearing heels and a suit. Her baby was nowhere near,
and neither was the man who had escorted her here. But
somewhere nearby she could hear the low cry of some
kind of cattle. She wondered if it had horns. Steven was
probably right—she didn't belong here at all.

She was still thinking the same thing much later, as
the sun was beginning to set. It had been hours since she
had eaten, or seen another human being. She had been
half-tempted to risk walking across the fields in search
of Steven, but then she had remembered what he'd said
about the weight of a cow.

And when a cow actually did wander right up next
to the truck, Jackie's eyes widened. "Nice girl," she
said, and the cow lowed, its nose nuzzling the door handle. She wished she could be one of those types who
could just reach out the window and pet a creature,
bringing it under her spell, but she couldn't.

She wondered if she would be awkward with
Steven's daughter. She didn't want that. It was important that this time should turn out to be something special, something different from what she had shared with
her own parents. Steven obviously adored his daughter.
She wanted to be an adoring parent, too. For half a second, she considered asking him to give her lessons, then
realized she couldn't when she had all but forced herself into his life.

At that moment she looked up and saw him moving
toward her, the clouds behind him lit up red and orange
and a deep purple. He looked tall and broad-shouldered

and tired, and the most familiar thing she'd seen in the past few hours. She had a terribly stupid urge to go to him. Instead she clenched her hands on the seat and stayed put as he gave the cow a brief pat, which sent it ambling away.

"Friend of yours?" he asked, opening the door.

"Bosom buddy," she agreed, "or jailkeeper. I thought maybe you sent her to make sure I stayed in the truck."

He raised a brow. "I'm not that devious, even though that would have been a good idea."

"Well," she said as he climbed inside, "all done? Where's your horse?"

"Ben and Hoagie are taking him back to the stable. Are you sure you're all right? This took longer than I thought it would."

She stuck out one high-heel-shod foot. "I stayed in the truck as you asked. Nothing broken. You can relax."

But he didn't look relaxed. "All right, we'll go meet Suzy, then," he said, and she finally understood.

He had just spent several hours working hard and now he had to take a woman he didn't like to meet his daughter.

Once again, she was the outsider.

"Let's go," she agreed, and he put the car in gear and started toward the house.

"Jackie?" he asked, and his voice was warm and low and husky in the gathering darkness. She wondered how many women had moved closer in the night when he'd called their names that way—which was just something she had no business whatsoever thinking.

"What?"

"Thank you for staying in the truck. I shouldn't have been so rude to a woman, especially a woman who's a guest. My mother would have tanned my hide if she'd known I had forgotten how to be a gentleman."

"You were protecting me."

"I was angry because I didn't know what the heck to do with you." His words brought back an old pain. No one in her family had ever known what to do with her.

"I should have taken you to the house," he confessed.

"No. No, you shouldn't have," she said, and she meant it. "When Suzy was born, you took on a duty to protect her. That might mean being rude to people now and then. I like the fact that you care about her that much."

"Every father loves his daughter that way."

"Not every father."

And suddenly she could feel him looking her way. She wished she could take back her words.

"I can't wait to see your baby's smile," she said, trying to change the subject. "Can't you drive any faster?"

"Don't worry, we'll be home soon," he said, and it was obvious from the affection that laced his voice that he loved his home.

She had never had a real home, but she didn't want to dwell on that. And she didn't want Steven to get that look in his eye again—the one that told her he was going to do his best to ferret out all of her secrets, and uncover all of her weaknesses.

"Are you going to let me inside this time?" she asked, teasing him.

"This time, yes. Come inside," he said, as he stopped the truck, and the look in his eyes hid more than it revealed. She'd just bet that any other woman would have fainted with desire if Steven Rollins had invited her to come inside his house.

But this woman knew that she was not a welcome guest. She had an agenda.

"Let's get started on our time together," she told him. "The clock is ticking."

Chapter Four

Suzy was on the floor, sitting amidst a pile of plastic blocks, one of which she was turning over and over in her little hands. She looked up when Steven and Jackie approached, and immediately her eyes lit up.

She lifted her arms. "Da!" she squealed, and he reached down and swung her little body high, cradling her against him.

"Hi, pumpkin," he said, dropping a kiss on the top of her dark, disheveled curls. "I missed you, sweetheart."

Suzy cooed. She turned big blue eyes on him, then shifted her gaze to Jackie. Immediately, she became more alert, her body tensing slightly.

"Oh, you are absolutely wonderful." Jackie barely breathed the words to the baby, keeping her voice almost a whisper. She didn't try to move close or touch Suzy.

"Buh," Suzy said, and Jackie raised quizzical eyes to Steven. He noted that the blue of her eyes was almost identical to that of his daughter's. Michelle, his wife, would have been happy. She had wanted her child to have blue eyes. She had wanted a lot of things, been adamant about them, and he hadn't always been able to come through.

"Buh?" Jackie asked him, mimicking Suzy's tone, and he had to smile.

He shrugged. "I don't know. It's just an all-purpose word she uses for anything or anyone new."

"Okay," Jackie said, her voice still a whisper. And suddenly she touched his sleeve. "I was so afraid she would cry. At least she didn't cry, Steven."

"Jackie, you're not a scary woman," he told her.

"You said I was hardheaded," and her voice sounded almost wounded.

"You are. It's not an insult. Hasn't anyone ever told you that before?"

He looked down on the dark, silky crown of Jackie's head, and she glanced up before returning her hopeful gaze to Suzy.

"Most people think I'm easygoing," she admitted.

"You?"

"Me. I almost always go along to get along."

He chuckled. "Then I must stir up something powerfully adverse in you."

She glanced up at him again, a slightly worried look in her eyes. "Relax," he soothed. "I don't mind a little sparring. I used to play football."

"I'll bet you were good at it." She looked at his bi-

ceps, and he felt a decidedly ridiculous masculine urge
to show her how strong he was by performing some gar-
gantuan feat.

Instead, he wrinkled his nose. "That was a long time
ago." And many fallen dreams ago.

"Buh?" Suzy said, and she snuggled closer. He
breathed in the sweet baby scent of her. She bopped him
with her wet building block.

"Little tyrant," he said, and Suzy giggled. She
smacked an awkward kiss in his direction. It landed on
the front of his cotton shirt, leaving a visible wet spot.

Steven heard a sound and looked down to see that
Jackie's eyes were misty. But she hadn't tried to touch
Suzy. She really hadn't made any attempt to communi-
cate with the child.

"Suze, sweetheart, this is…Ms. Hammond." The
name sounded much too formal for a one-year-old to
handle, but how on earth was he supposed to introduce
Jackie to his daughter?

Suzy stuffed a tiny corner of the huge rubber block
in her mouth and studied Jackie, just as if she realized
what Steven had said.

Jackie looked at his child with longing, as if she had
never seen anything more beautiful in her life.

For some reason he didn't completely understand, he
held Suzy out. "She doesn't bite," he said. "Not often,
anyway."

Jackie looked up at him as if he had given her dia-
monds, or a castle full of roses, maybe a garage stocked
with Ferraris.

"Are you sure?"

"I don't suppose you're going to do anything drastic with me here beside you."

She smiled and reached out. Suzy went into her arms. It was obvious that Jackie had held a baby before, but not often. She had the correct form, but she was still rather awkward. None of that mattered, though, because she looked like a woman having a blissful experience.

Until Suzy started to cry.

"Oh no, I've scared her, Steven." Jackie looked up with eyes as stricken as his child's.

And sure enough, Suzy was putting up a terrible howl.

Jackie held the baby out, and—hell, what could he do? He took his child and rubbed her back, soothing her.

"It's okay," he said, and he wondered if he was talking to his daughter or the distressed woman at his side with the trembling pink lips.

But Jackie didn't look as if she was buying into his encouragement. She fought whatever was bothering her and managed a tight smile, but her eyes were still sad.

"Time for Suzy to go to bed, I guess," he said, and he snuggled his child close, then turned her over to the waiting arms of Ms. Lerner, the nanny—a lean, tight-faced woman who loved his daughter to distraction.

Suzy went to her with no complaints. He turned to Jackie after his daughter had gone. "It will take time," he told her. But they both knew that time was something she didn't have much of.

Later in the night Steven awoke to the sound of someone stirring in the house. Throwing on a pair of jeans, he got up and went into the living room.

Jackie was seated on the couch in a high-necked baby blue quilted robe that covered her from neck to toes. Her hair was loose around her face. She looked very young, much younger than the thirty-one years that his attorney's file on her had indicated.

On her lap lay an open photo album, one that contained all the pictures he'd taken of Suzy this past year. When he took a step, and the floor of the old house creaked, she looked up.

"I'm sorry. Did I wake you?" she asked.

He shook his head. "I usually make a pass through about this time of night, just to make sure that everything's secure and Suze is all right."

"I was just…" She gestured to the book on her lap. "She looks like a happy baby."

"Smiles all the time."

Jackie bit her lip.

"Relax, Jackie. She's a baby. She takes time to get used to people. You didn't do any permanent damage. In fact, I'll bet she's smiling in her sleep right now. Want to see?"

An eager look turned Jackie's face luminous in the soft evening light. She nodded. "Please."

And so what could he do but hold out his hand? And what could she do but take what he offered?

Her skin was soft and pleasurable beneath his fingers, and he hadn't held a woman's hand just this way in a long time. He led her quickly to his daughter's room and silently opened the door.

They tiptoed in. Suzy wasn't exactly smiling, but in her pale pink sleeper, her dark lashes swooping across her cheeks, her dark halo of curls and her rosebud lips puckered sweetly, she was an angel on Earth. Her breathing was soft and even, and Steven's heart hurt to look at her, to know that she was his.

He glanced to his side. Lit by the faint light from the doorway and a night-light shaped like Winnie the Pooh, Jackie looked a bit like an angel herself. But a full-grown one with a woman's body. She gazed at the little girl with eyes that glowed, but when she looked up at him, he could see pain in their depths.

He led her from the room and closed the door.

"I want one," she whispered with a shaky laugh. "How lucky you are. It just melts my soul to look at her."

He raised a brow. "Did I say that you were a hard-headed woman? Maybe that isn't completely true."

She lifted her chin and gave him the look—the one that chased the need away from her eyes the way he'd intended it to. "I told you that I'm not hardheaded at all. And for the record, no one in the world but you has ever called me that."

"Oh yes, you told me that you were incredibly easy-going." He shook his head in disbelief.

She frowned. "Sometimes people even call me a marshmallow."

He laughed. "Sounds like a white lie to me."

"It's true. I almost never argue. I'm not a fighter."

"You're making that up."

"I am not." And she looked at him with a hint of indignation.

"I think you *are* a fighter when it really matters." And for some reason he didn't want to examine, he took a step into her space.

She gasped slightly.

He reached out and took her chin beneath his fingers.

"What are you doing?" Her voice trembled, but still she challenged him. Her lips were pink and full and incredibly enticing.

He leaned forward and took a taste. A small one, but even that was too heady. Her lips parted and he wanted more.

"Mr. Rollins?"

He raised his head and frowned, muttering an oath. "Jackie, you were supposed to tell me to stop. Maybe even stomp on my instep or punch me in the stomach."

She blinked. "You kissed me expecting me to attack you?"

He ran a hand through his bed-rumpled hair. "You haven't let me get away with anything so far. I was just going to prove that you weren't either a pushover or a marshmallow when it came to the important stuff, the stuff where you need to be tough and unyielding." It occurred to him that she was much more delicious and enticing than any marshmallow he'd ever sampled.

"I see. Then…if it happens again…"

He hoped to hell it wouldn't, because his body was already aching for a lot more than kisses, and that just wouldn't fly. "Don't hesitate next time," he said with a growl. "Just go straight for punching me in the gut. Not that I intend to let it happen again."

"No, of course not. You were just making a point."

He let the lie stand.

She bit her lip. "I—you just must have caught me off guard. I haven't done a lot of kissing and I was distracted. So yes, I promise to hit you very hard if you ever try to kiss me again."

"Good. I'll count on that," he told her.

But as she wandered off to bed he couldn't help thinking that it might be worth a few punches to feel her lips beneath his one more time.

Upon waking the next morning the first thing Jackie did was touch her lips. She still couldn't believe that Steven had kissed her. She wondered why he'd done it.

Had it been a punishment for coming in and forcing herself on his family? But she doubted that because he had told her that he expected her to retaliate by hitting him. Maybe he was just testing her. She just hoped he never found out that she had enjoyed his touch. The kiss had been so short, she had barely stopped herself from leaning close and twining her arms around his neck, pressing her belly to his hips…

If he realized that…well, it was bad enough that she knew, and she was certainly not going to dwell on the matter.

He had told her it wouldn't happen again. She had promised to hit him if it did. End of story. He had been making a simple point, and it was clear the man had no interest in touching her again.

Besides, all that had happened in the middle of the night, when everything was surreal. This morning was a new day. She was going to do her best to quietly win over the baby. It would require being patient and waiting. She had a lot of practice with both.

With a smile, Jackie climbed of bed, showered and

got dressed. She glanced in the mirror and was surprised to see a little color in her cheeks. For some reason that was disquieting. It made her look different from her usual colorless self.

"Silly," she told herself. "You probably stood in the sun too long yesterday morning. You'll have to watch yourself out here in the wide open spaces."

She headed for the kitchen. When she got there, Steven was at the table having his breakfast.

Jackie blinked and looked at the clock.

"Don't ranchers have to get up in the dark to do…whatever they do?" she asked.

"I've been up doing whatever I do," he agreed. "Now I'm having breakfast. Then I'll go out and do some more."

"Oh, that's good, then," she said, managing a smile. She certainly didn't want him to think that she wanted to spend time with him. Or that she was hoping he would kiss her again.

"You seem pretty pleased to be left on your own." His voice was somewhat grumpy.

"Oh…yes, I am," she agreed. "I have a plan."

He stopped eating. "A plan?"

"To win Suzy over. Everything's going to work out great, I think. You just go…do…"

"Whatever I do," he finished for her. And he got up from the table.

Jackie looked up as he stretched and all his muscles presented themselves to her. She pretended not to notice the awareness zipping through her body and bringing all her nerve endings to life. "Good day, Ms. Hammond," Steven said. "Suzy's still sleeping, but Ms.

Lerner's around. I'm sure she'll be plenty of company for you."

And then he slammed a baseball cap on that fine head of black hair and left the house, with the screen door bouncing behind him.

Jackie felt her smile slipping. It was as if Steven had a string attached to the sun and he was pulling it away with him.

Ms. Lerner came into the room at that moment with a sour expression on her face. "I'm not here to wait on you hand and foot. Let's get these dishes cleaned up before the egg dries on them. And don't be loud. You'll wake the baby.

"Mr. Rollins wouldn't like that. He doesn't like anyone who causes problems for his daughter or himself. You should probably know that. If I were you, I would think about leaving soon."

Jackie looked at the frowning woman. Oh great, another person who didn't want her here. It was certainly going to be a fun-filled day.

Chapter Five

He was darn well going to spend as much time away from the house as possible, Steven thought as he went about his work that day. What in hell had he been thinking kissing Jackie? And why couldn't he get that picture of her, wearing that pale blue thing with her hair all soft and tousled, out of his mind?

"Because you haven't had a woman in weeks," he reminded himself. If he were smart, he would just drive over to Miranda's tonight and take care of his problem.

But somehow he knew he wouldn't. It just felt...wrong. Probably because his mother had taught him too much about manners when there was company, he figured. Well, soon enough Jackie's two weeks would be up and he could get back to living the life of a bachelor.

And Jackie could get back to whatever social life she had, too. Probably some man back at the resort hoping she would let him into her bed soon.

Steven pounded the fence post he was working on a bit too hard.

"Want to talk about it?" Ben asked.

"What?"

"Why you're pounding that fence post so deep that somebody Down Under is probably feeling the vibrations."

"Just want to make sure it's solid," Steven grumbled, patting the very solid post.

"Yeah, I'd say it's solid, just like I'd say you don't like the fact that that pretty woman is up at the house romancing your daughter."

"You think she's pretty?"

Ben snorted. "I think she's got eyes that could get a man to do almost anything. That doesn't matter to me. What matters is what you're going to do about it."

Steven stopped pounding. He glared at his friend and foreman. "Not a damn thing. You know I don't get involved. Nobody knows better than you that my marriage wasn't ideal."

"Michelle didn't belong on a ranch, even if she *was* from around here."

"Exactly. It takes a woman who has always loved this way of life to settle down on a ranch. Besides, I don't aim high any more."

"Yeah, well you got your reasons. Getting injured and having to give up your football career and then your relationship with Michelle heading south and then losing her just when the two of you had started to make your peace…"

"Oh no, don't go down that road," Steven said. "I'm not going to start feeling sorry for myself. I've got a good life here with Suzy. Can't ask for more. I don't want more."

Ben laughed. "You want more. You just won't reach for it."

"Damn straight. And maybe the lady in question does have pretty blue eyes, but let's be honest. The two of us don't have a thing in common beyond a little heat and a lot of resentment. She's only here because of some mix-up when Michelle got pregnant, and I'll be glad when she's gone."

"Then you don't mind that Charlotte's probably putting her through the wringer?"

Steven pounded another post. "What are you talking about? Charlotte's a little reserved, but she's great with Suzy."

"Sure is, and she likes being the woman of the house. Isn't going to like sharing that baby she loves or that house she loves or giving up any of her authority."

Steven held up one hand. "Charlotte works for me. She wouldn't do anything."

Ben gave him a disgusted look. "This house and that baby are Charlotte's whole world. A woman coming here could change that."

"It isn't going to happen."

"Maybe not, but Charlotte doesn't know that."

Suddenly doubts pushed at Steven. Had he done something wrong, throwing Jackie and Charlotte together like this?

"Hmm, maybe we should take a short break and go have some lunch," he told Ben.

"Yeah, like you're going to get me to walk into the middle of *that*. Oh, no. You go on without me. I'm going to go find Hoagie and the boys. Hoagie's going to tell us all about his visit to town and why he came back wearing his underwear backward. We've been trying to get the story out of him all week."

Steven smiled. He had a small crew to help him with Rollins Acres, and some of them were pretty transient. But Ben had been here forever, and Hoagie was the closest thing to a son Ben had. The men got along, and that was a good thing.

It was one thing he didn't have to worry about, Steven thought as he headed back to the house. After talking to Ben, he half expected to find Jackie holed up in her room with the door locked and Charlotte holding a shotgun, but when he walked in the door, Jackie looked up from some papers on her lap.

He raised one brow. "Did you and Suzy have a good morning?"

She lifted one shoulder and looked at him warily. "Suzy is sleeping. I guess babies sleep a lot."

"Yeah, it seems that way. All that playing and laughing wears their little bodies out, I guess. It seems like Suzy is always busy when she's awake."

Suddenly Jackie laughed. "When she was up earlier, she actually smiled at me for a second. She didn't even cry." She said the words as if she had just won the lottery. And Steven, remembering his own reaction to his child's rapt expressions, figured that maybe she had.

There just weren't too many things better in life than having Suzy beam at him.

"So…you got to spend some time with her?"

"A few minutes. Babies have routines, you know, and it's important that they not be disrupted. It upsets their systems."

He heard her words, but realized that they probably had come straight from Charlotte's lips.

"I suppose they do, but Suzy probably wouldn't get too excited if we were a little more laid back about her routines."

"I don't know. Babies are so…fragile, so breakable and at risk. Aren't they?"

Not nearly as fragile as the look in this lady's eyes. But then he remembered how important her independence was. She probably wouldn't like him pointing out even one weakness.

"So you've had things to do," he said, nodding toward the papers on her lap. "Work?"

She shrugged. He noticed a smudge of dust on her cheek. On another woman it might have detracted from her appearance, but on Jackie's pale skin, it merely looked enticing. He stepped forward and rubbed his thumb across her cheek. Her skin was soft and warm.

She looked up with eyes that questioned him. He could see that little pulse in her throat jumping, urging a man to lay his lips right there.

Jackie took a deep shaky breath. She looked at her hand, which lay limply in her lap, and he realized she was wondering if she should hit him.

He couldn't quite suppress his smile. "You probably

should have, but now you're too late," he said as he stepped away.

She didn't ask what he meant.

"You had dust on your cheek," he told her, and immediately she lifted her palm and rubbed the place where he had touched.

"I was just—Charlotte and I—a ranch house takes a lot of work."

He frowned. "You've been working around the house? You're not one of my employees."

"No, I'm an intruder."

"You're a—" He tried to think of a word that fit. None did. "You're a guest."

She gave him a long look that called him a liar.

"I'm an uninvited guest if I'm one at all, and I don't mind that. I'd force my way in here again given the same set of circumstances. But that doesn't mean I'm going to expect you to pamper me. I want to be a part of things. That's why I'm here. To be a part of Suzy's life for two weeks, not a guest. That's the only reason I'm here," she said, and Steven considered himself warned. She was not here to let him touch her.

"Dust away then," he said, "if it makes you feel better. But don't feel you have to earn your keep."

She nodded, but he had a distinct feeling that she was simply humoring him, and that he might come in at any moment and find her down on her hands and knees scrubbing the floor—a thought that brought sudden heat to his loins.

What in hell was the matter with him? He really did need to get out more often.

"Come on," he told her. "I think I hear Suzy stirring."

Jackie's eyes widened. "You can hear something like that?"

He laughed. "Fatherhood heightens your senses. Sometimes I think I could hear her crying all the way across the fields if I didn't know that there was someone here taking care of her."

"I'm impressed."

"Don't be. It's a gift that comes with fear when you first bring a baby home. I was so scared that I would hurt her or let something happen to her in the night that I barely slept, lying awake listening for her. I understand most mothers and very few fathers are that way, but Suzy's case was special."

"You've had to be both mother and father."

"I'm not complaining. I like taking care of her."

"And she adores you."

He shrugged. "Babies are easy."

But at the pained look on her face he realized that babies weren't easy for Jackie.

"Come on, we'll go watch her wake up."

He led her to Suzy's room where Charlotte was already headed. "We'll take over, Charlotte. You go put your feet up."

"That's hardly necessary, Steven. You don't pay me to lounge around doing nothing." She looked pointedly at Jackie.

"I don't pay you to insult my guests, either, Charlotte," he said quietly. He ignored Jackie's outstretched hand, undoubtedly meant to stop him.

"I like being useful," Jackie reiterated firmly, addressing Charlotte rather than Steven. "I just want a chance to be useful with Suzy as well. It's only for a short two weeks, and I know I'll need lots of coaching and make lots of mistakes," she told the woman. "I appreciate that you're allowing me to try and fit in by helping with the house, and I'll be grateful for any pointers you can give me with Suzy."

Charlotte blinked, and Steven realized that the woman had been caught off guard. He should have known. Jackie couldn't succeed at her own business if she didn't have some very good people skills.

Giving a short nod, Charlotte left the room without speaking.

"You shouldn't have said that to her," Jackie said. "It made it look like I had tattled on her."

"You didn't."

"Yes, but she doesn't know that, and she probably found it somewhat humiliating to have you reprimand her in front of me. From the things she's said, it's obvious that she idolizes you."

He rubbed the back of his neck. "I know. I can't figure that one out."

"I think maybe she thinks of you as a son."

"You're kidding." He had never considered that. Charlotte was sixty and single. She had no children of her own.

"Of course I'm not kidding," Jackie answered. "I don't know Charlotte, but I know how I might feel if I were her. And she talks about you and Suzy with great pride. It's possible, and if it is true that she thinks of you as family, then it would really hurt her to have you criticize her publicly."

Steven ran his hand through his hair. "I hadn't considered that. And while I can't let her mistreat a guest, I suppose I've made my point. I don't want her hurt, and I'll do my best to smooth things over. Are you always this way?"

"What way?" Her blue eyes widened in apparent confusion.

"Observant."

Jackie shrugged and blushed a little. "Watching others was a hobby of mine as a child. It's a hard habit to break. Now, can I see our little one?"

The silence that followed was like the silence before an explosion. He stared at Jackie and saw that her color had heightened. She might have even said that she was sorry, but that didn't change a darn thing.

Had she really said *our* little one?

Steven took back any kind thought he had harbored about Jackie Hammond. She might be soft, she might be fragile, and she might appear to be sweet and good-natured, but all that was clearly a ruse—one he had nearly fallen for.

Jackie was worming her way in here and working to win over Charlotte. She was making him turn molten and soft and yielding.

At least he was almost yielding. Not quite, though. Because the woman was not to be trusted. Hadn't he read enough parental horror stories of people stealing babies, people who were otherwise crime-free but desperate to have a child?

Was that the kind of person Jackie was? He didn't know but he couldn't take any chances. Suzy was his life, his responsibility, his heart, and he would do anything, fight anyone who threatened her and her safe world in any way.

He didn't know whether Jackie could be trusted, but wasn't that the point? He *didn't* know, and yet she was here in his house for almost two weeks.

And what was he going to do to get her out of here?

Jackie couldn't have said what had made her utter that one little three-letter word if she sat up all night analyzing her thoughts.

Maybe it was the fact that she had been on pins and needles for days, and Suzy was the only person here who didn't seem to think that she was here to steal something or someone who didn't belong to her. It had been obvious from the get-go that Charlotte resented having her place as sole woman in the household usurped.

And Steven?

Jackie didn't even want to think about him. He was a confusing set of contradictions, clearly not happy to have her here—something she couldn't really blame him for—but also bent on being a gentleman, so that she kept forgetting that they were enemies.

She kept wanting him to smile at her, to like her.

That was a mistake. She had spent far too much of her life trying to win over people like her parents and Garret. She had learned how to be content with her own company and that of her many friends who, unlike her parents, didn't require her to jump through burning rings of fire for a little attention.

Some people just weren't worth longing for.

So why did her heart pound so hard when Steven looked at her? Why did she get misty-eyed when he insisted that Charlotte treat her fairly?

"Because you're an idiot who obviously has grown shallow," she told herself later in the privacy of her own room. "Because you're no better than any other woman, falling for a pair of broad shoulders and getting swept away by a man who knows how to touch a woman and make her burn."

Well, no more. She was here to see Suzy and to get to know Suzy. And she would not apologize for calling Suzy hers. She knew the little girl could never really be hers, but for just this short while she could pretend.

And Steven Rollins could just…well, he could just think what he liked, and he could certainly stay out of her mind, that's what.

For half a second she wished he would kiss her so that she could follow through on his orders and hit him, even though she had never hit another person in her life.

And then in the next second, she just wished he would kiss her.

Which was probably why the next few days were going to be long and hard and frustrating.

Chapter Six

The next day, as he went about the business of moving cattle, Steven tried to stop thinking about what was going on back at the ranch house.

After Jackie had uttered the fatal word yesterday, things had gotten more than a little stilted. He had taken her to Suzy's room, but there had been a sizzle in the air. He had been angry, and Jackie had been unrepentant.

At the supper table that night she had watched as Charlotte fed Suzy. To his amazement, Charlotte had glanced over at Jackie, who was studying the mealtime ritual, and had unexpectedly held out the spoon.

"Would you—maybe you'd like to feed her?" Charlotte had suggested.

No, Steven had thought, even though he didn't utter the word. Jackie had glanced his way, but he refused to say anything. He wasn't going to give the woman any

excuse to challenge him in the courts by telling everyone that he had denied her access to his daughter. Instead, he just meant to watch her very carefully.

Her lashes had floated down prettily, covering her
pale cheeks. "I'd—I'd like that," she told Charlotte.
"Show me how. You make it look so easy."

Charlotte had preened. "Nothing to it. You just stick
the spoon in her mouth and she does the rest. Even a
man can do it," Charlotte said, indicating Steven. "Show
her, Mr. Rollins."

And Jackie had looked at him as if he contained the
keys to the universe. For a brief second, his chest felt
tight and his blood pulsed quickly, a fact that only made
him angry at himself. He was half tempted to be sullen
and refuse the request, but Suzy was hungry and he
didn't want any arguments taking place in her presence.

He slid his daughter over carefully to face him. "Hey,
pumpkin," he said. "How 'bout a bite of peas?"

Suzy had smacked her lips and he had scooped the
food up, holding it close as she opened her mouth like
a baby bird. "Good girl," he said as she swallowed it.

His daughter smiled and glowed.

He turned and saw that Jackie was watching the two
of them as if they had just performed a magic trick. For
half a second he was tempted to think that he had mis-
judged her.

"She's such a sweetheart," Jackie said. "You must
feel blessed to have her."

He did, but he didn't like the covetous tone of the
lady's voice.

Still, he wasn't about to give her any excuses to accuse him of reneging on their deal. He turned over the spoon. She scooted close. The lily of the valley scent of her washed over him. Womanly, sweet.

He watched her closely.

She clutched the spoon as if it were a weapon capable of inflicting pain on Suzy. She scooped up a tiny bit of peas.

Charlotte snorted. "You'll be here all night like that."

"I don't mind," Jackie said. "I could do this all night." And she offered the food to Suzy.

Suzy laughed and batted at the spoon. Peas splattered all over Jackie.

Steven reacted instantly, picking up a napkin and wiping at the food that had landed on the midriff of Jackie's white blouse.

Immediately he realized his mistake. Her skin was warm. She gasped at his touch.

He dropped the cloth. "Sorry," he mumbled. He caught a glimpse of her troubled eyes, and he got up from the table and left the room.

For a few moments, there was silence. Then gradually he could hear sounds resuming, Jackie murmuring soothingly to Suzy. Suzy cooed in return.

She was wooing his child. He was letting her. All because he was afraid of his own reaction to the woman.

Steven took a deep breath and stepped back into the dining room. What he saw took his breath away. Jackie had Suzy in her arms. His daughter was resting on Jackie's arm, reaching up and playing with Jackie's hair.

Jackie kissed Suzy's little, flailing hand. She closed her eyes as her lips met the baby's skin and, for a moment, she looked as if she was in pain. But she quickly shook her head.

When she opened her eyes, she looked straight at him. A hint of pink climbed up her throat.

"I guess—I'm pretty new to all this. Holding a baby must be old hat to you."

He shook his head slowly. "It never gets old."

And then Suzy turned and saw him. She squealed and held out her arms to him.

He swung her high against his chest. He couldn't miss the look of longing in Jackie's eyes. She wanted his child. She coveted his daughter. Her lovely eyes were haunted and filled with loss.

He damned whoever it was who had found the paperwork that revealed the hospital's mistake. If he had never known—if *she* had never known—they wouldn't be here like this.

He wouldn't be wanting to comfort her, nor would he be desiring her and hating himself for that desire all at the same time.

If only they could get through this time without getting in too deep.

"I'd better put her to bed," he said.

For a minute he thought that Jackie was going to ask to come along, but then she simply nodded and bit her lip.

"This is much more difficult than I thought it would be," she said.

"You can say that again," he told her and then he turned and walked away. He resisted the urge to go back and comfort her.

* * *

The next day Steven left the house early and intended to stay out late. He didn't even go back for the noontime meal when the other men did. It was best for all concerned if he kept away. That way he wouldn't let his anger get the best of him—and he wouldn't let his desire get the best of him, either.

"That Jackie sure makes a mean lasagna," Ben said when he came back after lunch. "You should have had some. Probably none left by now."

Steven tried to ignore his friend. He mumbled something unintelligible.

"Yeah, and she sure has a way about her, too. Must have even soothed Charlotte, seeing as how she let the woman cook *and* watch the baby for a while."

A niggling sense of unease drifted in.

"You mean, watch the baby while Charlotte cleaned, right?"

Ben frowned, making his face even more wrinkled. "What's wrong with you? Charlotte needs to get out and get things done now and then. Usually she takes Suzy with her. It was probably a nice break for her to go to the store without having to worry about anything but the shopping."

The vague sense of unease deepened. It became a river of anger and distrust. "Are you telling me that Charlotte left my daughter alone at the house?"

Ben shook his head. "You know Charlotte would never do that. And I already told you that she left her with Jackie."

Which was virtually the same thing.

Steven swore beneath his breath. He dropped the tool he was holding, headed for his truck, climbed in and started the engine.

"What in hell are you doing?" Ben asked. "We're right in the middle of work."

Steven leveled a stare at his friend. "I just remembered that there's something I have to do. This won't take long."

Trouble or no trouble, courts or no courts, mistake or no mistake, he couldn't live like this. Jackie was a woman he had kissed, one he had desired, but none of that meant anything. It was just the way of a man without a woman in his life.

But Suzy…she was life and breath and everything to him. And if anything ever happened to her…if anyone tried to take her and disappear…

Life had taken so many things from him, but this…Suzy was different. He could not bear to think of anything harmful touching her.

He drove across the range like a madman, the truck bouncing and barely staying upright. When he pulled into the yard in front of the house, gravel flew in ten different directions.

Vaulting from the cab, he didn't bother shutting the door. Instead, he raced up to the porch and pulled the screen door wide.

"Suzy!" he bellowed, half afraid that she wasn't there. "Suzy!" The heels of his boots clicked as he moved quickly across the hardwood floor of the living room.

"She's sleeping," a soft voice called from the kitchen. "Or at least she was."

He could have taken Jackie at her word, but he ignored her and walked to his child's room, stepping more softly this time. Pushing the door back, barely daring to breathe, he peeked in and saw her there, her little face relaxed in sleep, the air whooshing in and out of her tiny lips in a gentle flow.

His knees felt as if they could buckle beneath him. He made his way back to the kitchen and plopped down in a chair.

The world felt like the inside of a black tornado. No, it felt like it might *after* a tornado had passed and he realized that he and his were still alive.

He dropped his head in his hands. The room was silent. Very silent. Dreadfully silent.

And that was when he looked up and saw what he had done.

Jackie's fingers felt cold and numb. Her body felt empty. Her heart was like a stone that had dropped to the bottom of the deepest, darkest part of the ocean.

There had been many times in her life when she had been misunderstood or ignored or chastised. But no one had ever accused her of doing anything criminal or deliberately hurtful, especially to a child.

He hasn't accused you of anything, she told herself. But she knew she was wrong. It was obvious by the way Steven had moved into the house in a panic that he had thought she had somehow harmed his child—or kidnapped her.

In a way, she couldn't blame him. After spending just a short time with Suzy, she coveted his child. She longed for one of her own.

Slowly, very slowly, Jackie took deep breaths. She tried to go back to the task she had been doing when Steven had arrived. She did her best to concentrate, to keep her hands from shaking.

Holding the knitting needles tightly, she concentrated very hard on looping the yarn around one, then inserting the needle through the loop and catching up the strand.

The needles clicked and she dropped the stitch.

Hot tears flooded her eyes.

Oh, damn.

She blinked and bit her lip and stared at the fallen stitch as if the world was ending. Clutching the needles even tighter, she tried to think what she was supposed to do in this circumstance. She knew, but she just couldn't seem to remember.

"It's nothing," she whispered. "Just a mistake. Fix it."

She tried. She really tried. And then a big warm hand closed over her own.

Jackie looked up through a mist into Steven's dark, unfathomable eyes.

For a moment, he looked as if he was going to apologize. Oh, please, no. If he did, she would know not to believe him. She wasn't sure she could keep the mist at bay if that happened.

"What are you doing?" he asked gently, bringing his other hand up so that he was holding both of her hands loosely in his, and the knitting lay abandoned on her lap.

She couldn't keep staring into his eyes. "I'm—I—I have a book," she said, gesturing with her head toward the book that lay open on the table. "I'm trying to teach myself to knit. I've never learned, but knitting…it's such a…it's the kind of thing that women do for those they care about. It's special because it comes from the heart. I thought…I just wanted to leave something special for Suzy when I go. I thought I might make a blanket."

They both glanced down at the tangled pale yellow yarn with the loose crooked stitches.

"That's a fine idea," he said, and his voice sounded a little broken. She wanted to look at him. She was afraid to look at him.

Instead, she shook her head. "I'm afraid I'm not very good at this kind of thing."

"You don't have to be. It's the thought that counts. It's always the thought that counts," he repeated. "Jackie, I—"

"Don't," she said suddenly. "Don't say what you're going to say. Don't explain. I know what this was all about. I know why you're here."

"I was wrong."

"No. You were being a father."

He placed one finger under her chin and gently forced her to look at him. "I was wrong," he repeated. "I should have known you wouldn't do anything to hurt her."

She shook her head and her skin slid against his. "How could you know?"

He twisted his mouth. "Well, for one thing, I did check you out, you know. After we talked the other day, I did a more thorough check. You're so clean you should squeak when you move."

She tried to smile, but then he brushed her cheek with his palm and all her thoughts disappeared.

"And I've seen the way you look at her," he continued. "That was the reason I was worried."

"Why?" The word came out on a broken sigh.

"Because you look at her as if she's everything you want in the world."

Jackie dared to look directly into Steven's eyes. They were dark and concerned and she felt both safe and totally discombobulated being this intimate with him. "I do want a baby," she said. "I don't think I ever allowed myself to think seriously about it before, but now…I just know. But, Steven?"

He waited.

"I would never hurt her, and taking her from you would definitely hurt her more than anything anyone could do. I wouldn't do that to you, either. I can't tell you how much I'm touched by the love you show her."

"A father—"

She cut him off by placing her fingertips gently over his lips, even though she realized it was a tactical error. Touching him this way made her remember that kiss. Still, she didn't want him to tell her about a father's duties. She knew that not every father felt a duty to his children.

"What you feel for her, how you treat her is special," she said slowly and carefully. "Believe me." And she refused to say more. "I honor that, and I wouldn't attempt to damage it, no matter how envious I am."

"You'll find a man. You'll make a child." His voice grew rough, his eyes dark.

"I don't think I want a man."

"Well then, you'll have a child another way."

She studied him. "I think I will, but that doesn't mean I'll ever forget this one."

And he took her hand from his lips, turned her palm and dropped a deep kiss on it. The sensation went through her. She trembled and did her best not to lean into him. "Thank you," he said.

"For what?"

"For caring about her."

"How could I not?"

He nodded tightly. "Then thank you for not insisting on more than the two weeks."

She swallowed hard, then also nodded. "It would be too hard…on all of us, but…I still have twelve days." And somehow she managed a tremulous smile.

"Then you should make the most of them," he agreed.

"I'm trying."

"I'll make it easier."

"How?"

He rose to his feet and drew her up with him. "If you want to really get to know Suzy, then you need to know the world she lives in, and not just here in the house. My daughter is being raised on a ranch. If you know what that entails, then in years to come you can imagine her here. Tomorrow I'll give you a tour of the rest of Rollins Acres."

"Thank you. I'd like that. I want to create lots of memories in the time I have left."

"Then we will."

His voice grew deep, and for a moment Jackie wondered what kind of memories he had once wanted to create, what dreams he had dropped. She wondered why he never wanted to marry again. He was a handsome man and a kind one with a touch…

Well, it was better not to think about that. But the truth was, he was the kind of man most women would want in their beds and in their lives. And he didn't want a relationship.

She wondered why, but she didn't ask. After all, she had her own secrets. And one of her secrets was that she enjoyed Steven's hands on her far too much.

Nothing I can do about that, she thought as he went back to work and she went back to knitting and babysitting. Besides, it was nothing to worry about. He was going to take her on a tour of the ranch. They would probably be riding horses or maybe just driving around in a truck.

Nothing romantic in that, so there wasn't a thing to worry about.

Chapter Seven

"This is going nowhere," Merry said to herself.

"What is?" Lissa walked up behind her.

"This...this *whatever* between Steven and Jackie. They both agreed that she needed to make some memories since she would be spending her life without Suzy. That certainly doesn't sound promising."

"Maybe another couple," Lissa suggested.

"No. Look at my hands, Lissa. Look at the wrinkles." Merry held out her bejeweled, slightly gnarled fingers.

"Some things just aren't meant to be, Merry. They've both lived difficult lives. You can't expect them to fall into each other's arms just because it's convenient for you."

"I know." Merry let her hands drop to her sides, a look of defeat on her face. "Ow!"

"Ow?"

"I felt a pain. An age related pain," Merry declared. "I do not like this getting old business. I refuse to let it happen, at least not when I'm still twenty-nine. I'm going to—"

"You're going to what?"

"I'm going to do something, something that will at least give Jackie and Steven a push. That's it! They just need a little push."

Her voice radiated excitement.

Lissa wondered what that meant. In the past it had not meant anything good…

Alone in her room that night, Jackie pulled out her cell phone and stared at it. She really should call Parris. Who knew what was going on with the business? And the business had been the one thing that had taken up all her time and thoughts until Steven Rollins had walked into La Torchére and turned her world upside down.

In a very short time, Hammond Events would be all she had, once again.

She didn't want to call. She didn't want to think about her normal life.

Suzy had lifted her lips for a kiss today after her nap. It had been the most awe-inspiring moment of Jackie's life.

Steven's touch still, hours later, made her skin burn and ache for a replay. She had never felt that way about a man's touch. She had never wanted a man's hands on her.

Now she kept wondering what she had said that had inspired that touch, what she could do to get him to look at her again as though she were something special.

It was pathetic. He had looked at her deserted knitting after dinner and pronounced it lovely.

"You did that yourself," he said, "because you wanted her to have something special to remember you by. That's amazing." And he had made her feel as if she truly had done something wonderful rather than completely mess up the project she had started.

No, she didn't want to call Parris and allow reality to seep in.

"But you're a realistic kind of woman, and it's probably a good thing to do what you can to get your head out of the clouds. Clouds always blow away," she reminded herself. "Or they don't blow away and they turn dark and drop rain on you."

She sighed. Hammond Events was her future. She had better not let her future fall apart—or let her father win again. If she did, she would have absolutely nothing to call her own when she left here.

And so she dialed. On the fifth ring, Parris picked up. "What?"

Jackie jumped, startled at her half sister's almost snarling tone. "It's Jackie," she said.

"Oh. Oh, I guess I knew that. If I had been thinking, I would have known that."

"I just called—"

"Jackie, I can't do this. You have got to come back."

"Parris, I can't."

"No, you don't understand. You have to. People keep wanting…things. What am I supposed to do with them?"

Parris sounded so uncharacteristically frightened that

if so much hadn't been at stake, Jackie would have left. "What kind of things?"

And Parris related what had been happening, all the crises, all the demands.

Slowly, Jackie sifted through what had to be done and how to do it, versus what could wait. She coached Parris until she was pretty sure her half sister had all the knowledge she needed.

"But can't you just come back? Really, I need help." There was a hint of something vulnerable in Parris's voice, but that couldn't be right, could it? Her half sister had never seemed vulnerable. That was just Jackie's imagination. The emotional nature of the past few days had her seeing things that didn't exist.

"Parris, believe me, you'll do fine. And no, I can't come back yet. Call me soon and tell me how all of this worked."

"It's not going to work. Nothing is working. If you don't come back, and maybe even if you do, everything is going to fall apart." And Parris hung up with an angry click.

Nothing is working.

Jackie hoped that wasn't an omen of how the rest of the week was going to go. Tomorrow she was going to step out on the ranch, and she was as ill-prepared for the world of ranching as Parris was for the world of business.

"But what can happen?" she coached herself. "I'm just touring. How could anything bad possibly happen?"

Jackie was a little jumpy, but eager, Steven noticed right away the next day. He wondered if she was jumpy because he'd been such a fool yesterday, touching his lips to her palm, or if she was just nervous about being out on the ranch. It had been obvious from the first that she was a city girl, and she looked very delicate. Being on a ranch probably wasn't her idea of a fun time, so he had to give her credit for guts. She had not complained once about his insistence on her coming to his home rather than the other way around.

"What do you want to see first?" he asked her, as he helped her into his truck.

She turned to him, wide-eyed. "I…well, I guess I don't exactly know. I don't really know the first thing about ranching, you know, except that there are cows and, I guess, bulls."

"Yeah, you pretty much need both to keep a ranch going." He tried not to grin.

A slight trace of pink crept up her throat. "Of course. And I've seen that you have horses."

"Yes, we don't use them quite as much as they used to years ago. The advent of trucks and SUVs has changed things, but we still work the cattle the old fashioned way, on horseback."

"So you must love horses like crazy? I would guess that a man who lived on a ranch would love them, wouldn't he?"

He smiled. "I don't actually know what a life without them would be like, having been around horses all my life. Although I probably don't think of them quite the way a person from the city would. A horse is not a pet. It's a partner, and a valued one."

"So you don't ride just for fun?"

He shrugged. "Sure, I do, when I have time. I'll—"

He had been planning on saying, "I'll take you some-day," but then he remembered that there wouldn't be a someday.

"How about you?" he said instead. "Do you ride?"

Jackie sighed. "I've never tried. That is, I've never even known a horse, really."

Steven couldn't repress a chuckle. "Well, then, I'll in-troduce you around the stable when we get back. For now, we'll just hit the high points of the ranch."

So he took her to the pond. "I have to confess that this is one of my favorite spots. Shady, green, peaceful. Someday Suzy will fish here," he said, and Jackie knelt and dipped her hand in the water.

"I can see it. Almost," Jackie replied. "She'll be much older then, of course. Walking, talking, skipping rocks." Her tone was wistful. Steven tried not to notice, but it was impossible not to.

He drove her to the outermost edge of the property, where Hoagie had torn the fence down, letting the cat-tle spill onto his neighbor's property.

"You certainly have a lot of fence," she said, eyeing the long expanse that seemed to wander straight to the horizon.

Steven shrugged. "A law was enacted back in the for-ties that required ranchers to fence cattle off all the roads. Makes for good neighbors."

"I'll bet it's tons of work to keep up that much fence."

"Sure is, but it's just the way things are. It's become a part of our normal duties."

Jackie shook her head as she eyed the miles of grass. "Normal to you is totally alien to me. I don't know a thing about ranching, and probably most of what I know is imperfect, colored by a lifetime of movies and books that didn't quite get it right. What kinds of things *will* Suzy learn as she gets older?"

Now here was a topic Steven had spent a lot of time thinking about. "She'll have fun, of course. Riding and roping and barrel racing can be exciting. But a lot of ranch work is tedious—repairing water lines and tanks and structures, including fences, keeping the vehicles working, getting rid of any invasive non-native plant species, such as soda apple, making sure the cattle are fed…" He trailed off. No doubt he was boring her.

"Don't cows just eat grass?" she asked, looking not at all bored.

"They do graze. But in the winter, even in this climate, we have to provide them with enough minerals. And even though we have a good vet, a lot of the day-to-day doctoring falls to us. Calves have to be helped into the world, and sometimes that's not easy. It's definitely messy. What's more, with so many animals, we have to make sure they're not carrying any diseases or parasites. Not everyone's favorite task." He figured he wouldn't even go near the task of branding, or explaining what it was like to artificially inseminate a heifer. It wasn't exactly the kind of thing most women bred in the city wanted to discuss in great depth.

"Sounds like a lot of work," Jackie said. "Like an entirely different world not far outside the cities and towns I've known all my life."

"I suppose it is, but it's the way we live," he said simply. "If you're born to it, you learn all the tasks as you grow up."

They both knew that Suzy would grow into this life, just as they knew that it was not the kind of thing someone who hadn't been raised on a ranch would find easy to pick up.

Suddenly Jackie smiled. "Aren't you going to tell me about all the warm, fuzzy stuff?"

He raised a brow. "Warm, fuzzy?"

Her smile grew. "You know, how sweet baby calves look or about the kittens the barn cats give birth to? Or the baby lambs."

Steven laughed. "No baby lambs here."

"No?" She sounded almost disappointed. He was half tempted to go out and find one somewhere just so he could tell her he had one, and that was saying a lot for a cattle man.

"Come on," he told her. "We'll go find something warm and fuzzy, if we can."

Who would have thought he'd be spending valuable work time trying to impress a woman who clearly had no business on a ranch? After his wife and her hatred of the land and this lifestyle, he had sworn he'd never even let another woman on his property who wasn't an employee.

But Jackie was already here and she was looking almost…eager.

"What exactly are you going to show me?" she asked.

He had no idea, but he figured that between him and Ben, they could surely find *something* on the ranch that would appeal to a city woman.

"Steven, that little heifer that we've been waiting on finally wandered off and calved." Hoagie had just ridden up on his horse to where Steven and Jackie were crossing the south pasture. "But there's a problem. The calf is too weak. Can't stand. I was just on my way to get a vehicle to bring him in, so I'm sure glad that you're here with the truck. The little mama isn't going to be too happy as it is."

Steven nodded. "We'd better take him fast," he agreed. "No point in making her suffer about giving him up any longer than necessary. Where's she at right now?"

Hoagie pointed and Jackie followed the line of his arm. A black and white cow, swaying, her head hung low, was nudging at a small bundle on the ground.

Steven gave Jackie an apologetic look. "Jackie, I—"

"Go on, you have to make sure she's all right. I'll be fine." And he turned the truck and headed across the field.

The heifer was lowing pitifully, nudging her barely responsive baby. There was muck all over the place. Jackie felt a lump in her throat. Just before Steven got out of the truck, she touched his sleeve.

"Will the baby be all right, do you think?"

He studied her face, then brushed a hand across her jaw. "I can't tell yet, but we'll do all we can."

Jackie watched as Hoagie neared the heifer and started waving his arms and dancing around, pushing at her and trying to distract her while Steven tried to get near the calf.

The cow let out a pitiful sound, but refused to budge.

A tight knot of pain crept up Jackie's chest as she watched the distraught mother. The poor thing. She was so worried about her baby.

Jackie moved forward, neither Steven nor Hoagie noticing her as they concentrated on their tasks.

"It's all right. They have to do this," she whispered, stepping close to the heifer. She placed her hand on the heifer's side.

"Holy cow!" Hoagie yelled.

"Jackie, don't!" Steven lunged forward, but he was too late. The cow turned at the sudden, unexpected contact and started to kick out.

Jackie quickly scooted back, landing on her butt in the damp mud.

Taking advantage of the moment, Hoagie quickly picked up the calf and carried it to the truck. Steven scooped up Jackie and did likewise.

The cow bawled piteously.

Hoagie laughed out loud as he climbed back on his horse. "Ms. Hammond, you sure know how to provide a distraction." And he tipped his hat and rode away.

Jackie tried to ignore her stinging bottom. It wasn't too difficult, since Steven was sitting there, tight-lipped and steel-jawed. "What in heaven and hell were you thinking, city girl? Do you have any idea what that hoof could have done to you?" he asked, as he threw the truck into gear and drove toward the barns.

Jackie bit her lip. "Not really. That is…I have some, a little, but in truth at the time, I just didn't think. She was so…"

"I know that." Steven's words were like sharp whips. "But, if all goes well, in a short while, she and her calf will be reunited. *You* might have been living with the results of your actions for a very long time. Or you might not have been living at all."

And then the silence fell like a sledgehammer. Jackie

wanted to apologize, but she didn't quite know what to say, because the man was absolutely right. She hadn't stopped to think. She hadn't stopped to consider the fact that both Hoagie and Steven had been doing this all their lives and knew what they were about. She had been concerned for the mother, but she had allowed herself to forget that Steven was a caring parent. He wouldn't be deliberately cruel. He was doing all he could to help his animals and make things right for them.

"It may not mean anything, but I truly am sorry I interfered," she somehow managed to say. "Ignorance is no excuse for impulsive behavior."

She thought she saw his hands tighten on the wheel. She was pretty sure that his jaw grew a bit more rigid. She saw his chest rise and fall as he took a deep breath.

Then he was silently helping her from the truck and into the house. He deliberately turned on his heel and helped Ben take the weak calf to the barns.

Jackie felt like a fool—but worse, she felt like an intruder. She had forced herself on Steven, had pushed herself into his life. How would he have felt if she had gotten kicked in the head? Despite his resentment of her, he wasn't an unfeeling man. To know that she had heaped guilt upon him...

She and Charlotte ate in near silence. Jackie was sure that sometime during the afternoon, someone on the ranch had filled Charlotte in on Jackie's actions. But, to her credit, Charlotte hadn't mentioned anything. Together, they got Suzy fed, and then Charlotte asked Jackie to watch Suzy while she got the baby's bathwater ready.

In a short while Charlotte returned and took Suzy away. Jackie started to go with them, but then she heard steps on the porch.

Charlotte looked back over her shoulder. "Maybe if you scoot in here real quick, you can make your escape. Steven takes ranch safety pretty seriously."

"I know," Jackie said, feeling an ache in her throat. "But I'll stay and face him." She was not a coward. She ran her own business. She dealt with difficult people all the time. But this time *she* was the one who had caused the difficulties. She refused to run from the harsh words Steven was bound to have for her.

She waited while he opened the door. She took a deep breath and squared her shoulders.

"Is…is the little calf going to be all right?" she asked. No point in simply waiting for the anvil to fall on her head. She didn't want him to know that she was nervous. Curling her hands into fists would do that. Instead, she pressed her palms flat against the sides of her new jeans.

Steven caught the action the way a hawk would catch the movement of a sparrow on the ground.

"He's fine," he said curtly. "We managed to get two pints of milk into him, and he's come around. He and his mother are off getting reacquainted."

Some of the tension drained out of Jackie. She realized that she had been half scared that her actions had inadvertently created a rift in the fabric of the ranch, that somehow the heifer and her calf would have their lives messed up by the unexpected drama she had injected this afternoon.

"I'm so glad," she said, and she couldn't help letting

her feelings show as she gazed up at him. "I was so worried about them."

For a second, Steven closed his eyes. Then he opened them again. He shook his head. "You know this is a ranch. Animals get hurt. They're not raised to be pets."

"I know that."

"Yes, but do you understand that Suzy will have to deal with that one day?"

"Yes." The word was tight.

"I hear the word 'but' in your voice, Jackie. Don't even go there. Suzy is my daughter. She's a rancher's daughter."

Slowly Jackie nodded. She knew what he meant. She would have to deal with the fact that Suzy would learn some things about life that other children didn't learn until they were much older.

"I'm sure you'll handle telling her the facts well," she finally said. "I can tell how much you love her. That will make it easier for her."

He studied her for a long moment, his dark eyes fierce and serious.

"Would you like to have a look at the calf?" he suddenly asked, holding out his hand.

Jackie nodded. She slid her hand in Steven's, knowing she was a fool to do so, because immediately she was aware of him as a man and herself as a woman. His hand was big and warm, his fingers locked loosely around her own. He had a way of making a woman aware of her body, of arousing her senses with just a look. And adding the sensation of touch only heightened everything.

She did her best to keep her mind on what they were doing—going to see an animal in the barn. Nothing sensual about that.

Yet when Steven stopped beside the pen where the calf lay against its mother, when he reached down and stroked it, murmuring softly, Jackie had never seen anything so gentle and touching.

"Just an animal?" she asked.

He shrugged. "Nature is fascinating," he admitted. And he took her hand and held it out toward the animals. "She's stopped fretting now that she has him back and he's all right. You can touch now, and she won't mind."

Jackie let her fingers sink into the thick pelt of the calf. "He's so warm," she said with wonder.

"New life," Steven said. "It's miraculous, isn't it?"

She suddenly looked up from her preoccupation with the calf. "How did it feel when you first held Suzy, when she was new?"

He gazed directly into her eyes, and suddenly Jackie remembered that his wife had died when his child had been born. "I'm sorry. Don't answer that. It was an insensitive question."

"It was a natural question. And yes, I'm not sure I was really in control of my emotions that day. But later…later I marveled at how tiny yet strong and vital she seemed. I fell in love from the first. I wanted to protect her in the worst way, and maybe losing her mother only made the desire to protect her that much stronger."

"Was your wife…was she a rancher by birth?"

"Actually, she was, but she never liked the life."

But she understood it, Jackie thought. "I'm sorry about today," she said.

"It's all right," he told her. "You were just responding to your emotions. Don't do it again," he told her, and he helped her to her feet and silently led her back to the house.

When they went inside, he didn't let go of her but walked her to her door—as if to make sure that she was locked tightly inside her room, where she couldn't make any dangerous mistakes.

For long seconds he stared down into her eyes. "I've never seen a woman with such delicate skin," he said, and then blinked as if he had surprised himself. "The elements here wouldn't be kind to you."

She nodded. "I've always had to be careful in the sun, because I burn. And Steven?"

He waited.

"About this afternoon. I won't do anything like that again," she said softly just before she closed the door. But she wasn't sure she was talking about the incident with the calf. Steven Rollins stirred her. Every time she looked at him, she felt too much, whether it be good or bad. That couldn't go on.

She passed the mirror on her way to bed and glanced at herself. Her eyes looked somehow luminous in a way they never had before—dreamy, some might say, and she had never been a dreamy kind of person. She had always been the nurturer, the fixer, trying to make things right with her father, with her mother, sometimes with Parris.

"Even with a sad cow," she mused, realizing that she had been at it again. Fixing things.

"Well, that's who I am, after all," she said, and she sat down and pulled out some paperwork that Parris had e-mailed to her that day. Two more donors were getting cold feet.

Jackie took out her cell phone and called them. She fixed things. Now if she could only fix things so that she and Steven Rollins weren't constantly butting heads. Or if only she could stop thinking of him as a very desirable man.

"Well, time will heal that," she told herself. "Today is living proof that I don't belong here. From now on, I'm going to concentrate exclusively on Suzy and forget that the man even exists."

"Did you hear that?" Merry asked herself, gazing into the cell phone from which she heard Jackie's words as she uttered them. "She apparently can't wait to get away. She wants to forget that Steven even exists. What if she succeeds?"

She frowned and punched the off button, watching as Jackie's features faded away.

"Well, that's just too bad. Jackie can't succeed, because if she does, I fail. I have got to make sure that she remains aware of Steven as a man. Very aware. And I know just how to do it, too."

Chapter Eight

When Steven came into the house for lunch the next day, Jackie was down on the floor, on her stomach, building a tower of blocks. Suzy sat on Charlotte's lap and watched her.

"All set," Jackie said, and smiled at Suzy.

Charlotte let Suzy go, and she tottered over to the tower.

"Uh," she said as she swatted at the red, blue and yellow tower. Blocks flew everywhere with a mad clatter.

Suzy laughed and patted her hands together.

"Oh, you are so clever," Jackie declared, smiling at the child and pulling her close for a cuddle. Suzy lifted her lips for a quick kiss, then grunted, pointing to the blocks.

"Again?" Jackie asked with a laugh.

"Gen," Suzy agreed.

"You're spoiling her rotten," Charlotte drawled, but

she didn't seem all that upset. In the past, Charlotte would have exclaimed at the mess or worried that a block might break something, even though they never did.

"She's unspoilable," Jackie declared. "Aren't you, pumpkin?" she asked, using Steven's pet name for his child. A quick stab of fear—and something else—hit him. He shoved it away. Jackie was here for such a short time, and she was trying so hard to fit in. He had a feeling that after yesterday's incident she wouldn't go near the rest of the ranch unless he gave her the okay.

He wondered if he hadn't been too harsh on her, but no. The memory of Jackie falling back and that lethal hoof aiming for her head still made him want to double over with fear. He didn't want to examine that fear too closely, either.

"A natural reaction to anyone in danger," he muttered to himself.

"What?" Both Jackie and Charlotte turned around, noticing him for the first time.

Oh yeah, like he was going to tell them what he had been thinking about.

"Are you teaching my daughter how to break things?" he asked, with a mock accusing look.

Jackie gave a laugh of satisfaction, a sound that was pure music. "There's no teaching involved. She's a natural, and very good at it, too. You should be proud of her. I'll bet she'll learn how to take a cow or a calf or a bull—or whatever it is that you work with—down with very little effort."

He grinned. "I think we'll start her on calves. Little ones made of pink terry cloth and stuffed with cotton.

A bull would be a bit much for a one-year-old, even one as talented as Suzy Q. Come give daddy a hug, pumpkin." And Suzy left Jackie and toddled to him with her arms outstretched. Love and gratitude filled his heart, just as it had every day since she'd been born.

He looked at Jackie and saw the longing in her eyes. He remembered how she had called Suzy her baby and how they both realized that this was only a temporary arrangement—one that would be over forever once it ended.

"You're good with her," he acknowledged, and returned his daughter to Jackie's arms.

The lady lifted one delicate shoulder as she placed her cheek against Suzy's. "She's a sweetheart. Any woman would be good with her."

Yes, but this woman had shared her genes with Suzy. He stared at the two of them, their blue eyes so similar, their dark hair so alike. He wasn't sure, but he thought they might even have the same smile.

"Smile," he almost said to Jackie, just so he could check. Or maybe because she lit up so radiantly when she smiled.

"We brought in a new mare today," he said, instead. "Got her from Ned Battleman. She's very gentle, maybe even a little shy. Would you ladies like to see her?"

Charlotte gave him a look. "I been looking at horses and men who raise horses all my life. You bring in a trapeze artist or a NASCAR driver or even an interior decorator, I'll come look. A horse just doesn't interest me all that much. I'm taking a bubble bath and soaking my feet."

And she stalked off.

Jackie blinked. "I thought Charlotte liked ranches and ranchers and horses."

"She does," Steven said with a smile. "She just used to date Ned Battleman until they had a falling out. I'm not sure what it was about, but she's had nothing to do with him since. Charlotte will be out to look at the horse in her own sweet time, preferably when no one can catch her cooing at it. You game?"

"Yes, but…" Jackie gazed down at Suzy, who had tired herself out and was now half-asleep on Jackie's shoulder.

"We'll go tuck her in," he whispered. "I'll take the monitor with me, so Charlotte can have her bath. If Suzy so much as blows a bubble in her sleep, we'll be back in a flash."

Jackie gave a nod. "Let's go."

"Well, that's more like it," Merry whispered to herself. "A horse. A horse could be useful. I can't tell people what to do. The restrictions Lissa has placed on me forbid it, but I might be able to whisper to a horse."

She studied the visions on the screen of the cell phone.

"It won't exactly be easy, but I might as well give it a try."

She clicked the cell phone shut.

"After all, what do I have to lose?" She started to answer her own question, then thought better of it.

It was better not to even think about some things. If a person thought too long and hard, they might get frightened and never take action of any kind.

And she had to take action.

In the end, it wouldn't hurt Jackie and Steven, anyway.

* * *

Jackie tried not to think about how nervous she was. She hadn't actually ever been near a horse. She had certainly never ridden on one, and she didn't want to look stupid or awkward. Steven already called her a city girl, which was only the truth. She didn't want him to think she was completely inept.

"Which is just completely stupid," Jackie muttered as she went upstairs and pulled on her new boots. Why should she care what Steven thought of her?

Just because he had been concerned about her when he thought the cow was going to kick her? Just because he didn't care if every man on the ranch caught him cooing to his baby? Just because he made a point of making all his employees feel like family? What did those things matter? He was still a man, and one who had declared that he had a certain disdain for a relationship with a woman.

"So what? You're not going to have a relationship with him," Jackie told herself. "He's just taking you to meet a horse. And you are going to learn something." Surely she couldn't do any worse than she had with the knitting. She glanced down at the growing yellow cloud of knitted yarn she had produced. It certainly wasn't very shapely, but she just couldn't give up.

And she wouldn't give up here, either, no matter how scared she was of a very big animal with very big teeth.

Jackie pulled her hair back into a low ponytail, plopped a white baseball cap on her head, took a deep breath and set off to learn more about Suzy and Steven's world.

She was marching so determinedly that she almost didn't see Steven, who was outside on the porch, lounging against the wall of the house. He had his ankles crossed and his hat tipped down to protect him from the sun.

"Whoa," he said, in a low soothing voice. "Over here. She's not in the barn. We've got her in the far corral right now."

Jackie turned and faced the corral in question. A milky white horse was delicately walking around, tossing her head, her mane flowing proudly about her.

"Oh, she *is* beautiful," Jackie couldn't help declaring. "Steven, I don't know one little thing about horses. You know that, right?"

He gave her a small grin. "I'll bet you know something."

She lifted one brow. "I know you ride them and that they have an interesting history with man, but…you know what I mean. I don't have any firsthand knowledge."

"I didn't expect you to. It's not a sin."

She nodded and gave him a slight smile. "Thank you. That's probably saying a lot coming from a rancher. My point is that even though I don't know much about horses, even *I* can tell that this one is special. Why did that man, that Ned you were talking about, get rid of her?"

Steven shrugged. "She's barren."

"And yet you bought her."

"She's gentle. I needed a gentle horse. For Suzy."

But Suzy wouldn't be old enough to ride this horse for a long time. Jackie had the strangest suspicion that Steven had brought the horse here *now* because he had a horse-ignorant guest in his home. She wouldn't say that, though. He would surely deny it, and maybe it wasn't the truth, after all.

"Anyway, she's very lovely. Can we go closer?"

"Absolutely. The boys and I have all been over to Ned's and we've ridden her. She's as gentle as a horse gets. You couldn't ask for a better horse to initiate you into the fold."

"Fold?" Jackie frowned, confused.

"The members of the I Love Horses society," Steven whispered. "It's a very select group. Membership is practically a requirement for anyone visiting a ranch."

"Ah, I see. Is there a secret handshake?"

"Nope. Just have to give the horses a chance to win your heart. Come here. I'll show you."

He led her to the corral and pulled back the gate, letting the two of them inside before he shut it again. "Now we're going to walk up to her real slowly, let her catch your scent and get used to it."

Steven took Jackie's hand and began walking toward the horse, whispering softly. His palm was warm against Jackie's, his touch commanding. She struggled to keep her reaction to him at bay. There was something about this man—about the sensation of having her skin against his, about the way he soothed the horse—that made her want to lean close to him. She stopped herself.

"Look, she's studying you. She's fascinated," he said.

And yes, when Jackie looked into the horse's intelligent eyes, she felt an instant sense of communion.

She and Steven moved closer, until he was standing next to the horse and she was facing it.

"What's her name?" Jackie whispered.

"Shiloh."

"It's a pretty name. Hello, Shiloh," and Jackie took one step closer.

At that moment, a breeze drifted across the hereto-fore breezeless sky. For a moment, Jackie felt disoriented. She almost thought she heard something, something that hadn't come from Steven or Shiloh.

Ridiculous, she thought, but Shiloh was suddenly dancing around, her ears twitching.

The breeze drifted through again.

"What the heck?" Steven said, as Shiloh began to whinny and roll her eyes. She bucked a bit and he reached out a hand.

"It's okay, girl. What's wrong?" he asked.

And then the breeze came again, more distinct this time, with more vigor and sound.

Shiloh's ears twitched very hard and she started to swing in a circle, ramming her body hard against Steven's and knocking him in a small arc across the space that separated him from Jackie.

Jackie saw the movement as if it were happening in slow motion. Shiloh's huge body connected with a thud against Steven's shoulder. She heard the sickening sound of his flesh being hammered, and saw his body being hurled across the dirt of the corral.

He landed against her and, as she fell back, he caught at her, looping his arms around her. Curling her into him as the momentum of Shiloh's push hurled them to the ground, he protected Jackie from the fall, twisting his body and taking the hard pounding of the impact himself.

Jackie thought she saw him wince slightly, but he

quickly recovered. The horse had retreated to the other end of the corral, and Steven immediately began running his hands over Jackie, sliding his palms from her arms to her legs.

"Are you all right?" he whispered urgently.

She couldn't speak at first.

"Jackie, talk to me," he commanded. "Are you hurt? Where does it hurt?"

It didn't hurt, but having him touch her this way, lying against him like this, was overwhelming. He was all warm male, wrapped around her, taking command of her, touching her gently.

"Jackie?" Deep concern laced his voice. She knew his sense of responsibility and she didn't want to cause him to worry.

"I'm...okay," she somehow managed to say. "Really."

"Good." And to her surprise, he got up, scooped her into his arms and carried her from the corral, setting her on her feet only after they were outside the corral. But he was frowning.

"Are *you* okay?" she asked, and she gently touched his shoulder. He didn't make a sound, but she felt him flinch.

"Come on, I'm going to wrap that for you," she said. "Right now."

"No, later," he said.

"Steven..."

He turned to face her. "Jackie, I don't know what happened back there. I swear to you that I've never seen Shiloh act like that, and I've seen her at Ned's a thousand times over the years."

"I believe you," she said solemnly and sincerely.

"Why should you? I've been mean as sin to you since you came here."

"You've tried to be mean. You're not always very good at it, though."

He raised his brows at her. "Are you saying I'm soft?"

She reached out and felt his very hard muscle. "Inside, I think you are. A bit," she conceded. "You don't do mean very well. At least not for long. And you love your daughter far too much to hide the caring part of you. So yes, I believe you about Shiloh."

"Doesn't change things. I wanted you to learn that a horse doesn't have to be a big, scary creature. I wanted you to at least leave here knowing that Suzy would have a fulfilling time growing up on a ranch. I bought Shiloh for the two of you."

Tears clogged Jackie's throat. She managed to nod somehow and keep the tears from moving any farther up the line to her eyes. "Thank you," she finally managed to say.

"But I can't let Shiloh near you now, and I don't want you to leave here without having at least one experience of riding a horse."

"Sure you can. It's okay."

"It's not okay. I'm a rancher, dammit. My daughter will grow up on a ranch, and you will be the mother of a rancher. I don't want you to worry that some horse is going to trample her."

"I won't." But her voice wasn't as strong as she would have liked. "I believe you'll protect her."

"And I want a picture of you on a horse, so that she can see it," he said.

Oh gosh, those darn tears. They were going to mist her eyes for sure now, she thought, swiping them away.

"Will you?" he asked gently.

"Will I what?"

"Will you let me take you up on my horse? I won't put you on Shiloh, which was my original intention, and I won't put you on a horse alone, which was also my original intention. But I want you to see what it's like, to let her see that you tried it once, even if it's just for a few seconds."

And what could she say? He wanted Suzy to have a picture of her on a horse, even though she was her mother in biology only. "Yes," she said, a bit too heartily as she nodded hard. "Yes."

He barely moved. "Ben," he yelled, and the old hand came out from the barn.

"I got ears. You don't need to bust my eardrums."

"Can you or Charlotte get a camera? I want a picture of Jackie on Blue."

"On Blue? Holy moly, Steven, that animal's twice as tall as her."

"I know. I'll hold her. I'll keep her safe." And he said the words in a hushed voice, a sacred promise.

Jackie nodded as Ben stomped off to get the camera. She followed Steven as he saddled Blue and led him outside.

The horse *was* huge, and black—a giant among horses. But Jackie looked up into Blue's eyes and saw the communication that passed between man and horse. That trust and faith had been built over years. This horse would not betray this man.

So when Steven helped her up onto the horse, in the brief seconds before he swung up beside her, she kept her eyes on Steven. She refused to give in to the fear that would have engulfed her on any other day.

"I've never been on a horse," she conceded. "Nothing other than the pony rides when I was a girl, and those little ponies were always so sad. I worried about them after I saw them."

"Good girl," Steven told her, and she wasn't sure if he meant the way she had sat on the horse while she waited for him, or the fact that she had showed concern for the captive ponies walking in endless circles.

And then he looped his arms around her, and she forgot everything except his warmth, except how natural and safe it felt to be this way. For a few minutes in her life, she could look daring, and she had never been daring. For a very short time, she could look like she belonged to this way of life when she had never really belonged anywhere.

"We're going to walk a little," Steven whispered near her ear, and it was all she could do to keep from leaning back against him, to keep from tilting her head so that his lips could touch her.

"All right," she said a bit shakily.

"Are you afraid? Tell me if you're afraid," he whispered again.

She was afraid, very much so, but not of the horse. She was afraid of what she was feeling and wishing for right now.

Jackie swallowed hard and felt Steven's chest brush her back. His legs encased hers, warmth and sensation skimming up her thighs where Steven's body touched hers.

"I'm all right," she told him. "I'm not afraid." And, she decided, she wouldn't be. This was a good feeling, a wonderful feeling. If she was only going to have it once in her life, then she would enjoy it, and she would not feel guilty.

"I'm wonderful," she said, and she laughed.

His arms tightened about her. His legs brushed more intimately against hers. "You're amazing," he said. "You really are."

"In what way?"

She felt him shrug, the slow and subtle slide of his body against hers a delicious tug of sensation. "I come to you out of the blue, tell you that I have a child you helped make and insist that you go along with my terms. You walk into a lifestyle that is completely foreign to you. You put up with Charlotte, at least until you won her over. You put up with me. You agree to my terms all the way, nearly get kicked by a cow, flattened by a horse, manhandled by a…man—"

"And kissed," she reminded him. "You kissed me." Jackie didn't know why she said that. She just felt like remembering that moment.

"I did that, too," he said, his voice turning deep and thick, his body pressing closer against hers. She could feel the vee of his thighs where they cradled her buttocks. A shiver ripped through her.

"Does it bother you to remember that?" he asked her.

She turned a bit in his arms, as much as she could, which wasn't nearly enough. "Would it bother you if I told you that I liked it when you kissed me?"

He didn't answer at first. Jackie felt the warmth seeping up from her throat. Why on earth had she said that?

And then his hand came up and slid against her stomach. He stopped the horse and turned her head just enough to catch her lips. His heat and the force of his touch scalded her, thrilled her, made her want more.

"It bothers me," he said thickly when he let her go, "because I liked it, too. And we both know I can't go there. I have Suzy, and you're the one woman I can't allow myself to desire."

She closed her eyes. She knew that, of course. They were Suzy's biological parents. They couldn't play love games or games of passion. A child was caught in the middle. There was no future for Jackie here. Steven and Suzy couldn't have her here. She didn't fit, and neither she nor Steven wanted a long-term anything. So Steven and I can't do this, Jackie reminded herself. We could complicate things for Suzy.

"You're right," she said softly. She did her best to keep her shoulders from slumping.

"Let's take that picture," Steven whispered thickly. "For our daughter's sake."

And his words, his acknowledgment of her as a mother, brought quick tears. She blinked furiously. When Ben snapped the picture, he had to take it again because Jackie was blinking so hard. In the end he took several shots at Steven's behest.

And when Steven helped Jackie off the horse and she began to walk toward the house, she knew she and Steven would never share this kind of intimacy again.

She had just ridden her first horse, and it had been the most exciting, fulfilling experience she could remember.

"Never again,' she whispered out loud.

"What?" Charlotte asked as Jackie moved into the house.

"I said, where's my knitting? I have to finish the blanket."

Charlotte looked at the pathetic yellow mass. "I'll say one thing. You're not a quitter," she said.

But Jackie knew different, because she was going to have to quit thinking about Steven. She was afraid she was going to start dreaming about him at night and wanting him all day long. And what would she do then?

Chapter Nine

"I can't believe you did that." Lissa had her hands on her hips, and she was glaring at Merry.

Merry, in spite of her almost thirty years and her ancient appearance, bit her lip like a child. "It certainly didn't happen the way I planned it."

"Steven could have been severely injured. For that matter, so could Jackie."

"I just don't understand it. The horse wouldn't listen."

"Maybe she was a sensible horse."

Merry might have responded angrily in the past, but today she just looked worried. "I think I scared her."

"Obviously."

"And I didn't really help Jackie and Steven's cause. They're more determined than ever to ignore the attraction they're feeling."

Lissa gave her godchild a concerned look. "Merry?"

"It does seem a bit hopeless," Merry admitted.

"Things don't always work out the way we've planned. You can't force every person to fit the mold you've made for them."

Merry gave a bitter laugh. "That seems obvious. I just—"

"What?"

"I don't know. They seem more unhappy now than they did when I first threw them together." Her voice sounded sad. She walked away, her shoulders slightly slumped.

Lissa's eyes widened. Merry had just showed a hint of concern for someone else.

"But things don't always work out the way you've planned," she repeated, this time to herself. "Don't get your hopes up."

She wouldn't. A week had almost passed, and Merry still had five couples to go. No progress had been made, and the clock—and the curse—wouldn't wait forever. Not for the first time, Lissa regretted that darned curse, but there was nothing she could do about it. Once it had been set in place, it was irreversible unless the terms were met.

And now it didn't seem as if they would be, just as it didn't seem as if anything but regrets and bittersweet longing would come out of this time between Steven and Jackie.

Steven was both dreading and looking forward to the next few hours.

He turned to his daughter. "Ready to go try and make

some new friends, pumpkin?" He held out his arms and Suzy lifted hers, waiting for him to pick her up.

"I don't know how you can stand to go to that place," Charlotte said with a snort. "The noise alone gives me the heebie-jeebies."

"I thought Steven said he was taking Suzy to a play-group," Jackie said, looking up from her knitting. "You love children, Charlotte."

"It's not the noise of the children I hate," Charlotte said.

Steven laughed. "It's not that bad."

"Hmpff. I'll just bet it isn't," Charlotte agreed, though her voice was laced with meaning.

Steven frowned. "And it's not like that."

Charlotte gave him the look. She glanced back to Jackie.

"What?" Jackie asked, and it was clear that she didn't have a clue what Charlotte was talking about.

The dad-blamed thing was that Charlotte was right, Steven thought. He gave Jackie a speculative look.

"Don't even think of doing that to her," Charlotte said.

"Doing what?" And now Jackie put her knitting aside.

"He wants you to protect him from the mommy brigade."

"Now Charlotte, that's not true, and you know it. It's just—I don't go there to meet women. I want Suzy to get a chance to meet kids. Sometimes it just doesn't work out the way I want it to."

"He means that the women are trying to rip his shirt off while he's trying to organize a game of Simon Says with the kids."

"That never happened."

"Well, maybe not, but you lost a button." Charlotte held up her sewing.

"It's a stupid idea to ask Jackie to do something like that, anyway," Steven admitted. "And it's unkind. I apologize," he told Jackie, "for attempting to take advantage of you."

Jackie gave a quick jerk of her head. Steven cursed his poor phrasing.

"What I meant was that I was going to use you as a shield so I could get some playtime in with Suzy. We don't do enough of that, at least not with other kids," he admitted. "I know she's a bit young for playing in a group, but I just want her to get used to being around other kids, since she'll never have brothers and sisters. Silly, I know."

"You're inviting me to Suzy's playgroup?" Jackie asked.

"Honey, he was trying to bamboozle you," Charlotte pointed out.

"Nonsense. I am a businesswoman. I have had the best attempt to bamboozle me. This wasn't the same. Still, I didn't quite hear an invitation." She reached for her knitting again.

Steven laughed. He dropped to one knee and reached for Jackie's pretty hand. "Ms. Hammond, would you do me the honor of accompanying me to the Kids Kamp-around Play Group?"

Jackie fluttered her eyelashes theatrically. "Why, Mr. Rollins, since you asked so nicely, I believe I will accept your kind invitation." She grinned and set her knitting aside. The yellow yarn mass was growing in both bulk and shapelessness. "A woman can take only so much humiliation with the needles in one day. When do we leave?"

Steven chuckled. "Right now would be good. My carriage is your carriage," he said.

"The pickup truck?"

"Definitely."

"You charmer, you."

"I try real hard, ma'am." But he didn't have to try to joke around with Jackie, he realized. It just came naturally. She made it easy. Too easy, because he found himself wanting to be with her too much, to touch her too often.

And today? That excuse about the women keeping him from Suzy and the kids?

Well, no one kept him from his daughter if he didn't want to be kept from her. And he didn't.

Besides, no woman had posed a danger to his sanity or strength of purpose since his marriage had failed years ago.

Except for the woman right at his side.

Jackie Hammond was ten times more dangerous than any of the women in his daughter's playgroup, and he had just failed another test with her. He had vowed to keep his distance, yet here he was, mooning over her again.

The playgroup met in an empty meeting room of the local municipal building. Blue and red padded mats had been set up at one end of the room, and there were lots of shelves full of toys that looked as though they had been well-loved for many years.

Jackie walked in beside Steven, who was carrying Suzy. Suzy immediately started bucking.

"Da, da, da," she cried as if to get her father's attention.

"Want down?"

"Dow," Suzy agreed, sticking half a hand in her mouth and nodding, those big blue eyes solemn and sure.

Steven set her on her feet, and she headed toward the mats in the awkward but cute as heck zigzag motion of the newly walking, squealing with delight.

"Party time," Jackie murmured, and Steven laughed.

"As close to it as we get around these parts. No group birthday parties for the kids yet," he admitted.

"Birthday party? Why, I was just thinking that we needed to get the children together more often," a tall, tanned blond woman said, moving very close to Steven. "It's so good to see you, Steven. You missed last week."

For half a second Steven's eyes rested on Jackie. "I had some business last week," he said, and Jackie understood. He had been trying to decide what he was going to do about Suzy's biological mother.

"Well, you're here with us now, and that's the important thing. You add so much to our group," the lady cooed with a smile.

Steven didn't smile back. "This is my guest, Jackie Hammond," he said. "She's staying out at the ranch for a couple of weeks."

"Oh?" the lady said.

"Beverly Darvish," he said to Jackie, and Jackie stepped forward and held out her hand in one smooth motion, a practiced smile on her face. This woman clearly wasn't thrilled to see her, but then the business world had prepared her for those moments when people weren't inclined to be hospitable.

"Pleased to meet you, Ms. Darvish," she said.

"Are you a relative?" the lady asked, barely touching Jackie's hand, a tight frown on her face.

"No, I'm—"

But at that moment several other women bustled up, interrupting Jackie's speech. Just as well. Who was she going to tell them she was? What would Steven call her?

"Jackie is my guest," he said firmly, his tone admonishing the woman for her rudeness.

A small murmur went through the women. It almost sounded like a small growl, Jackie thought, but that was probably her imagination. It was not her imagination that the women didn't like her being here.

Well, she had dealt with difficult clients before. "Excuse me, ladies, but I think Suzy needs us." Which was a bald-faced lie, since Suzy was contentedly jabbering with another baby who was examining a pink teddy bear.

"Fatherhood calls," Steven agreed, and he took Jackie's arm in an exaggerated courtly gesture—just like something out of a historical romance—and led her away toward the baby corner.

When they were far enough away that she could whisper without being overheard, Jackie leaned her head close to Steven's. "Don't they have husbands?"

He shrugged. "Most do. That group doesn't. It's not a big deal. Usually."

Maybe not, but when Jackie glanced over her shoulder, she saw Beverly glaring at her.

"Don't worry. I don't think she can shoot fire this far," Steven said with a wink.

"Hmm, I was more worried about the darts she's hiding in her purse and the bull's-eye I've grown on my back."

"No problem," Steven said, and he placed his palm on her back as they continued to move toward Suzy.

"Oh, that'll work," Jackie said, barely suppressing a giggle. "Now they'll really hate me. They already think I'm after you."

"But you're not."

"No," she said soberly, hoping she wasn't lying again. "I'm not." And if she were after him, she wouldn't have any kind of a chance, anyway. Steven didn't want a wife. And if he did, there were several in that group who were much prettier than she was. That shouldn't have bothered her, but somehow it did. The little nip of pain was even worse than the one she had felt a few years ago, when Garret had switched his allegiance from her to Parris even though Parris had no interest in him.

These women had a definite interest in Steven. And why not, she thought, watching him kneel down between the two babies.

"Who wants a horsey ride?" he asked.

The baby-jabbering grew more excited. Both Suzy and the little boy tried to climb on Steven.

"Okay, okay, I think I can fit you both, but Jackie is going to have to help me. I don't want anyone sliding off and getting hurt."

Immediately Suzy started tugging on Jackie's hand. "Ja," she said, which was the closest she had ever gotten to Jackie's name—something which brought an instant lump to Jackie's throat.

She gave a tight nod and started to lift Suzy onto her father's back, then reached for the little boy.

That sweet little wide-eyed innocent instantly gave Jackie a worshipful look. The magnitude of it stopped her cold for a second.

"You're doing fine," Steven encouraged. "Absolutely perfect." Jackie looked at him and saw that he was studying her intently. "Perfect," he repeated. Between the three of them she had never felt so adored in her life.

She smiled at Steven and dropped to her knees. "Okay, you two," she said. "Up you go. Hang on." And as Steven waited on all fours, Jackie helped both children on. She wrapped Suzy's arms around the little boy's waist and then Jackie held his hand as Steven began to move slowly around the mat.

The little boy crowed and bucked. Suzy squeezed tight.

"What's your friend's name, Suzy?" Jackie asked, knowing that Suzy wouldn't understand the question, but not wanting to talk over the children.

Suzy smacked her lips. The little boy squealed again. Jackie leaned down. "Name?" she asked, touching the child's arm.

"Name," he repeated.

Jackie blinked.

Steven started to chuckle.

"Uh-oh," Suzy declared as both children started to slide.

Immediately Steven halted. "Jackie, darlin', help us," he said. "Or we're going to take a tumble."

Immediately Jackie scooped the babies into her arms and righted them on Steven's back. "Whoa, that was close," she said with exaggerated mock relief, brushing a hand over her forehead. "Want another ride?"

The children squealed with delight.

"Thank you," Steven said as he began to make the circuit of the mat again. "It may be only a short drop to a heavily padded mat, but a horse has some pride. This horse hasn't dumped a rider yet."

"What a special father you are," Jackie said suddenly, the words seeming to come out of nowhere. Her own father would have never risked his dignity this way. He'd never even considered the fact that his child needed and craved his attention. Or if he had, he had dismissed her needs as inconsequential in comparison to his own.

Steven stopped and stared at her. "Nicest thing anyone has ever said to me, I think," he told her, and for some reason she just couldn't look away. She reached out as if to touch him.

Suddenly there was a stirring on the other side of the room. Beverly was clapping her hands. "Story time, everyone. Mrs. Lucy is going to read everyone a story. Come on, now. Find a spot."

Jackie half expected a stampede, but she hadn't reckoned with the personalities of one-year-olds. Half the children ignored Beverly completely and kept doing what they were doing. Others simply moved from one activity to another. One little girl started crying piteously. Parents started scooping up children and carrying them over to the story area.

Steven waited while Jackie helped the two little ones dismount. Then he took the little boy by one arm and looked at Jackie. "Why don't you hold Suzy on your lap while they read the story. She gets antsy and likes to cuddle halfway through. At least she does if she's with someone she likes a lot." His tone implied that Suzy liked her a lot, and that he was okay with it.

It was the closest to a gesture of total acceptance that Steven had ever given her, and Jackie couldn't stop herself from touching him this time. She placed her hand on his arm. "She's really lucky to have a father like you."

He rotated his arm and slid his hand to take hers. "Thank you for coming here with me today. Now...about that story?"

"I love stories. Read them all the time," Jackie said with a smile, and she reached out her hands to Suzy.

But at that moment, Beverly Darvish barreled in, nearly knocking Jackie down as she stepped between Jackie and Steven. "Steven, I saved a seat for you, just like always. This would probably be boring for you, anyway," Beverly said, barely turning her head to aim the last comment at Jackie before turning back to Steven. "Come on, now, you've got Davis. I'll just take Suzy." And she swung Suzy up in one arm and linked her other through Steven's. Immediately she started moving toward the story area. Suzy was twisting in her arms and trying to look backward to where Jackie was. Her little face was puckered up in a look of sheer distress.

Jackie glanced at Steven and saw that his eyes had turned hard and cold. He didn't move a muscle at Beverly's urging. Instead, he easily freed his arm and gently placed the little boy down on the nearest mat, making sure the child was safe and happy. Then he took his daughter from Beverly, who flinched at his quick and graceful movements that so easily reversed everything she'd just done.

"That was real nice of you to offer, Beverly," he said, his voice laced with steel, "but in case you didn't hear me right the first time, I told you that Jackie is my guest. I don't ignore my guests, and I don't exactly appreciate someone practically knocking her down without so much as a word of apology. You'd better run along now. I think you're already missing story hour. *Red Riding Hood* is just about halfway to Grandmother's house. You wouldn't want to miss the ending. It's pretty good. That wolf is pretty pushy, but the woodcutter doesn't let him get away with anything."

And then he smiled at Beverly and winked, just as if he'd been kidding all along, but the smile was a bit thin.

Beverly blinked and opened her mouth. Then, without saying another word she turned and walked away, her back ramrod straight.

"Are you all right?" Steven asked Jackie, who had jumped back hard when Beverly had all but shoved her out of the way.

No, I will never be fine, because I can't get my bearings with you, Jackie thought. He caught her off guard in one way or another time and time again. No one had ever truly stood up for her before. No one had ever expressed any true interest in her well-being.

She nodded slightly. "I'm fine," she said. "She didn't really knock me down."

"Well, if she had, I got the impression she wouldn't have noticed or cared. Come on. Care for a story?" He looked toward the area where almost everyone had gathered.

"Oh, I'm afraid I've had a bad experience with that one," she said softly. "I've always loved fairy tales, but *Red Riding Hood* put me off of hiking in the woods for weeks when I was a little girl."

"No wolves here at Kids Kamparound," he said with a smile.

"No," she agreed, for no one could call a man who wasn't interested in a woman a wolf. "But I have an idea. When we're done here, take me to a bookstore, and I'll find a new story for Suzy. I'd like that. But…" She looked down at the cheerful little boy who had gone back to his pink teddy bear. He was hugging the bear and nearly falling over with drowsiness. "Who does *he* belong to?"

Steven chuckled. "He's Mrs. Lucy's, the storyteller. He's such a good baby that she knows someone will always take care of him. In another minute, when the story ends, she'll come get him and take him home. In the meantime, I'm going to find him a crib and tuck him in. He needs some snooze time. All babies do."

But Suzy was looking as bright-eyed as ever. "Suzy doesn't seem sleepy at all."

"She thrives on all this company. It's as if she forces herself to stay awake through the whole thing, but when we get her home, she'll go out almost right away. Happens every time."

"Ah, a little social butterfly," Jackie said, kissing Suzy's hand.

"Just like her mother," Steven said, and then he froze.

So did Jackie.

He rubbed the back of his neck and started to open his mouth.

"Don't," she pleaded. "It's okay, really. I'm sure that something happens in the womb, some kind of communication that scientists haven't been able to analyze yet. Even though your wife died, and even though Suzy came from my eggs, I bet your wife still passed on a part of herself to Suzy."

The look that Steven gave her was fierce, dark and far too difficult to read. "Let's go," he said.

"What? Did I say something wrong?"

But he was already gently picking up the little boy and carrying him to a crib, where he covered him and stroked his cheek softly before carrying Suzy out of the playgroup.

Jackie followed. She arrived at the car just as Steven had finished putting Suzy in the car seat.

"Did I say something that made you angry?" she asked. "If I did, I'm truly sorry."

He rose to his full height and took two steps that brought him right beside her. "You didn't say anything wrong," he admitted.

"Then why do you look so angry?"

"I'm not angry with you. I'm angry with me because you said something very right. It's not the first time, either. You say things, you do things, that intrigue me, and I don't want to be intrigued. Can you understand how it is?"

Oh yes, she could understand all too well. He was standing so close she could breathe in his scent, could feel his warmth. She could remember how he had put Beverly in her place just because she had been rude to his guest. Jackie barely managed to nod.

"You say that, but I don't think you really can," he told her, and he raised one hand and slid it beneath her hair, behind her neck.

She swallowed hard. "I—no one has ever stood up for me before," she said suddenly, her heart speeding up to a trot. "That intrigues me. I don't like it much, either, even though I'm grateful for what you said to Beverly."

But he frowned. "What do you mean, no one has ever stood up for you before?"

She shrugged. "Nothing, really. I just—my father didn't like having children. He and my mother were divorced, and she blamed my existence for causing him to leave."

Steven uttered a word Jackie couldn't quite make out. She was pretty sure that it wasn't a nice word, and that he had muttered it beneath his breath so that she and Suzy wouldn't have to hear him swearing.

"I'm not complaining," Jackie quickly said. "I got over all that a long time ago, and it's okay now. I'm just explaining."

He continued to stare at her, tilting his head to study her more closely. "It's not okay," he said in a deep rasping voice. "But you stand up like a little soldier and just take what life gives you. You duke it out and make your way. You take the time to notice the little things, the important things. You donate your eggs to a woman who could never have a child without them, and then go so far as to speculate that that woman surely gave her baby something *in utero*. You said it because you felt that it mattered to me."

"I said it because I thought it might be true," she said, half breathless as his hand slid gently higher on her scalp. It might be true, she thought. The woman who carried the baby might well give her child a part of herself through her bloodstream. Wasn't it possible? But, she admitted to herself, she had done her wondering out loud because she had thought that he needed to hear it. He had lost his wife and, his life had been invaded by a woman he had never thought to meet—the egg donor. He had given to her, Jackie admitted, and she wanted to give back what she could. She breathed out slowly.

"I said it because it might be true," she insisted softly. "It could happen. Babies are so much more than genetic material."

"Oh, but that genetic material can be very important," he said, his voice dipping deeper, his thumb beginning a slow caress up and down a sensitive inch of her neck.

Jackie swallowed hard. "I...I...maybe."

"You want me to stop touching you?"

She closed her eyes. "Yes. No. I don't know. You intrigue me, too, and I don't like it, either."

"I know. I wish to heck it wasn't so, Jackie darlin', but the truth is that there's just something about you..."

She felt the warm, minty drift of his breath. Her eyes flew open. She gazed up at him and then she reached for him. She rose on her toes. "There's a lot of something's about you. I don't like it at all," she declared hotly. And then she kissed him. Hard.

"I don't like it," she repeated, half to herself. "And I

don't want it. Now let's go home and forget all about this." She didn't even berate herself for using the word home—he knew what she meant.

She just wished *she* knew.

And she wished, she really wished, that she could stop thinking about Steven as a man she liked, a man she desired. How much easier it would be if they could just go back to arguing and being adversaries.

But that couldn't be good for Suzy, Jackie thought.

I guess I'm just doomed to burn for the man until the day I leave. And then I'm going to turn my back on Rollins Acres forever. I'm going to try to forget.

But a part of her knew she would never forget, not the child and not the man. The best she could do for now was to distract herself and keep her mind off Steven and on the reason she had come here.

"I can do anything I want to if I put my mind to it," she told herself later that day. "All I need is a really good plan."

Chapter Ten

Steven had apparently taken her words to heart, Jackie thought two days later. Since she had kissed him the man had barely come near her other than to let her know where he could be reached or to let her know in small, subtle ways that he trusted her with his daughter.

"I've talked to Charlotte," he had said just that morning as he was going out the door. "She agrees that you should have more of a chance to spend time with Suzy. So if you want to take her to the playground or for a walk, I just want you to know that I'm not going to be dogging your footsteps. I don't want you to feel you have to be looking over your shoulder to see if I'm watching your every move."

"But I'm not," she whispered to Suzy as she squeezed a dollop of baby shampoo into the palm of her hand and luxuriated in the feel of the little girl's tiny scalp beneath her massaging fingertips. "Your daddy has hardly even been around lately, sweetie pie. How could I even begin to think that he was watching my every move? He's off somewhere with his horses and cows, I expect." Jackie knew that her voice was a little wistful. She couldn't escape the fact that she missed Steven's deep voice. She missed him, even though she had no business doing so.

But at that moment Suzy looked up at Jackie, blinked and then splashed both palms in the bathtub, sending water flying everywhere.

Jackie jumped but held on to the baby. "You little imp," she said, smiling at Suzy. "Did you do that on purpose to make me laugh?"

Suzy cooed and smiled and looked totally innocent.

"Yes, well, serves me right for letting my thoughts drift, sweetheart. I shouldn't have been fretting about your daddy, anyway. It's probably better if I stay here and he stays with his cows. At least I can't do anything stupid this way." Other than spend all her time missing a man she had no business missing.

"Cowww?" Suzy said, dragging the word out. "Moooo."

Jackie laughed. "Yes, moooo," and she puckered her lips to accentuate the word.

At that moment she looked up to see Steven standing in the doorway, watching them. Jackie realized that her lips were still puckered. She quickly straightened them.

Steven's gaze dropped.

She looked down and realized that the water had

made her white blouse cling to her body. She breathed in a deep gulp of air and looked up into Steven's fierce, dark eyes. But all he did was give her a quick nod, then move away.

Once again, she and Suzy were alone. This was what she had wanted when she came here, wasn't it? It was still what she wanted, wasn't it?

Carefully, she scooped the baby out of the tub and wrapped her in a clean white towel. She hugged Suzy to her.

"You're all that matters," she whispered to her child. But in her heart she knew she lied. She was starting to care for things she had no business caring about. She was starting to realize that her coming here might have been a mistake in many ways.

But if she was going to be able to go back to her own life and be happy, she needed to find a way to turn things around and make these two weeks end light and easy. Somehow, there had to be a way.

He was doing his best, Steven told himself as he moved about the house later that night. He had not gone near Jackie, even though it meant time away from his daughter. Jackie only had a short time with Suzy. He was going to try very hard to let her have it in peace, with no distractions.

But as he passed by Suzy's room, he couldn't help peeking in. Maybe he could just give his child one quick good-night kiss and then leave.

Slowly, silently, he pushed open the door, not wanting to wake her if she was already asleep. And there they were. Jackie was seated in the rocker, Suzy on her lap, a book held so that both of them could see.

"And then when the handsome prince realized that not only was the princess beautiful, but also a pretty good barrel racer who was terribly smart and very handy with ranch chores," Jackie said, "he decided that he really wanted to get to know her better. What do you think of this story so far, sweetness?"

Suzy cooed sleepily. She pointed her little chubby fingers at the picture, then rubbed her eyes.

"Yes, that was one pretty on-the-ball prince, don't you think? He knew that a woman is more than just a lot of pretty hair and eyes," Jackie added. "Not that there's anything wrong with pretty hair and eyes. Yours are very nice, but I can already tell that you're smart and funny and so much more. The prince saw that in the princess, too. And look, see, she realized that he had some good points, too. He could ride and rope and flex his muscles, but he also knew how to cook and wash his own dirty laundry. Not bad for a guy, huh?" And she hugged Suzy and dropped a kiss on the top of her head.

Well, heck, Steven thought, holding his laughter in check with some difficulty, how was a man supposed to ignore that? He cleared his throat.

Jackie jumped. His lovely visitor looked up then, her eyes big and round, just like Suzy's. The only difference was that Suzy was smiling. Jackie was turning a delicious shade of pink that dipped right down the vee of her white blouse in the most enticing way.

Reluctantly, and with some difficulty, he reined in his errant thoughts. He let her off the hook by raising his gaze back to her eyes. "Nice story," he said, not able to keep from smiling. "I don't seem to remember it reading quite that way the last time I looked at it, but I'm sure the author is long gone and won't mind a bit of embellishment."

Jackie lifted one shoulder and gave him a reluctant and sheepish smile in return. "Oh, it's a great story just as it is, but…"

"You like a man who can cook and wash his own dirty laundry?"

"I…well, I've never actually had to do either of those tasks for a man."

"But if you did, it would be nice if he could step in and do the right thing?"

Jackie shrugged. "We were just being silly." She cuddled Suzy, who was looking drowsy, as she rose from the chair. She tucked the baby into her crib and gave her a kiss before returning to Steven.

"What *do* you look for in a man?" he asked, rephrasing the question.

"I've told you I don't."

"But if you did?"

She bit her lip. He gave her points for not reprimanding him for butting in where he had no business. "I guess I don't really know," she said. "This was just a story. I was just playing it by ear. Suzy's going to be raised in the real world. Even though she can't really understand, I wanted her to know that there's so much more to a person than their looks. Life can be fulfilling on many levels."

He let himself wonder what he had avoided thinking about until then—what would happen when Jackie left the ranch?

"Is your life fulfilling?" he asked suddenly.

She didn't hesitate. "Yes. I have my work."

"That's all?" He hadn't allowed himself to wonder too much about a man in her life. She had said she didn't want one, and he believed her. But things could change if the right man came along. He wondered if that would happen and what she would do then.

He waited for her response, and finally she stared directly into his eyes. "Work can be very rewarding. Mine makes me happy," she said firmly.

That was a good thing. She should be happy. But he didn't want her to be alone. He didn't want her to be with a man, either. Add those two together and they didn't make a stitch of sense.

"That's good," he told her. "I want you to be happy." And without thinking, he took a step closer.

"I will be," she said, but her voice was quiet and choked. Somehow he didn't believe her. He remembered how she had looked holding Suzy while she read. She was going to have to give up that part of her life, such a precious part. It was the only way. And he realized how he would feel if he had to give up holding his daughter and reading her fairy stories and tucking her in at night.

"What a mess," he said beneath his breath.

"I know. I shouldn't have come, I think," she said, and her voice was almost a whisper. "I might have to leave soon, anyway. Parris called me this morning. She's having problems."

"You don't have to leave yet?"

She shook her head vehemently. "No, not yet."

"Good." And against everything his mind was telling him, ignoring all the warning bells he had been listening to for days, he stepped forward and placed his hands on her shoulders. He felt her softness beneath his fingertips and he was lost.

"Jackie," he whispered, and then he pulled her close and placed his lips on hers.

She moved into him as if she had been born for this moment. Her body fitted to his in just the right way.

He tasted her and found that she was warm and sweet and just as he had remembered. She was perfect, and he couldn't keep from nuzzling her. He placed one palm just beneath her breast.

"You can tell me to stop and I'll try," he somehow managed to say, wishing she would and hoping she wouldn't.

"No, I can't. I can't," she said on a whispered cry as she returned his kisses. "I want to, but I can't. Help me, Steven."

And that was enough. She didn't want this, not really, and he couldn't force it on her.

Slowly he released her. Gently, he stroked her hair away from her face.

He looked down at her and saw that he had broken her, at last, now that he didn't want to. He was going to hurt when she was gone, but at least he would still have Suzy.

She would only have...what?

"Do you and your sister get along? Are you close?"

She blinked as if she didn't understand him. Then, finally, she shook her head. "We barely know each other. She's my half sister and we weren't raised together. My father divorced my mother to marry her mother. Not long ago, he deeded one of his failing businesses to both of us, so we do our best to get by with each other, I guess."

The jerk, he thought. What kind of a father was that, to give her only crumbs? And he was sure that was the way it was from things Jackie had let slip before. She only got the bits and pieces, and now she wouldn't even get that with Suzy. When she returned home she would, essentially, be alone, he thought, wanting to swear but not allowing himself to. And she would only have two weeks of memories of Suzy. This kiss—and all the others they had shared—was proof enough that the two of them could never see each other again after these two weeks. They couldn't risk the aftermath, or hurting Suzy.

"I'll have your bed moved in here," he said suddenly. "You can spend the next few days in her room. You can be with her as much as possible. I'll give you pictures of her. I'll give you what memories I can."

She looked up at him with stricken eyes. Her fingertips were on her lips. He hated himself for hurting her.

"Thank you," he thought he heard her murmur, but he couldn't be sure. He was already headed out the door.

"It's the bunkhouse for you, Rollins," he told himself later. "You just keep your distance from Jackie until the day she has to leave."

Yes, he would do that, because he could see that he was hurting her every time he touched her. He was taking advantage of the fact that she was already missing Suzy and not fully in control of her emotions. He wasn't in control of his emotions, either, but that didn't matter.

Jackie was at risk. So if he had to, he would ask Ben to set him straight if he tried to go near her again. Ben was no fool. He was a very wise man, and he would do what was best for everyone concerned. Thank goodness for that.

"Every time those two touch, things just seem to get worse," Merry said, glancing into her cell phone. "I don't like this turn of events at all. Is the man really going to the bunkhouse? What's that all about?"

But she listened in as Steven talked to Ben.

"Good idea," Ben said. "She's a pretty little thing, as sweet as they come, and I don't blame you at all for being tempted. But if she doesn't want to get married and you don't want to, either, then the smartest thing you two can do is stay far, far away from each other. If you don't, that baby is going to get caught in the middle and get hurt."

"I know that," Steven said, and somehow his voice didn't even sound like his own. "That's why I'm counting on you to remind me to be smart if I forget."

"Don't worry," Ben said. "I'll make sure the two of you stay apart."

"No!" Merry cried, and she threw the cell phone across the room. Then, realizing that she might have broken her only link with Steven and Jackie, she rushed over and picked it up off the floor, her knees aching as she did so.

"I need a miracle," she whispered. "Just one little miracle." But where was she going to get one? And how was she going to keep Ben from ruining everything when he was there and she was many miles away?

Chapter Eleven

Jackie put Suzy down to play with her family of stuffed animals and plopped down on the floor next to her. But within seconds Suzy was crying, reaching out to be held, her little face tense and scared.

"What's the matter, sweetheart?" Jackie asked, crooning to the baby, swaying as she picked her up and held her.

Suzy stuffed her fist into her mouth. She quieted a bit, but not completely.

What am I doing to you? Jackie couldn't help thinking. Suzy was starting to cry for her, to depend on her. And, worse, Steven was staying away from this little girl who absolutely adored the ground he walked on. All because of me, Jackie thought. I'm wedging my way in here, making Suzy dependent on me, keeping her from her daddy.

"That's just not right," she murmured as she turned her

face to the child's velvety cheek and gave her a kiss. And so she walked the floor with Suzy, rocked her, sang to her. Eventually, the little girl drifted into a restless sleep.

"Do you want me to put her to bed?" Charlotte asked.

No, Jackie thought. I want to do everything for her. I don't want to be apart from her. But that wasn't right, either. She had to start weaning herself from Suzy and Suzy from her. And Charlotte had given up so much of her own time with the child. The woman loved this baby so much, she must have missed all the close contact.

"Thank you," Jackie said, and she even managed a smile.

"She gets to you, doesn't she?" Charlotte asked, nodding to Suzy whose body had gone limp in Jackie's arms.

"I never knew it would be like this."

"I know just what you mean. Single women miss out on some things, don't we?"

And the two women gazed at each other knowing that here, at least, they shared an unbreakable bond.

"She misses Steven, I think," Jackie said. "He's been so busy."

Charlotte looked away, but she gave a nod. "He had me fix up a picnic basket for you and Suzy for when she wakes up. I've got directions to a good shady spot when you're ready to go."

"Just the two of us?"

"Sounded that way."

"Where does—what have the men been doing for lunch? When I first came here, they sometimes came to the house."

Charlotte shrugged as she eased Suzy from Jackie's

arms. "Oh, they're men. I cook for them, but they just haven't come in lately. The food doesn't go to waste. I just save it for supper. Anyway, I wouldn't worry. They're pretty good at taking care of themselves when they have to. Heck, they'd eat rocks if that was all there was."

"Maybe they just don't have time to come in. Maybe I should bring them something to eat."

"Maybe you're asking for trouble."

The two women exchanged a look. "You're most likely right, Charlotte. I've been known to do that. Look how I forced Steven to bring me here against his wishes. But I can't enjoy your delicious picnic lunch if I think Steven is staying away so he won't disturb Suzy and me. And I'm pretty sure that's what he's doing. What do you think?"

"I think you're going to do whatever you want to do no matter what I say," Charlotte grumbled, but she didn't really look mad.

"You think I'm wrong?"

Charlotte laughed. "No, I think you're right, but I don't think Steven's going to just let you lead him here. You need ammo."

Jackie laughed at that, and it was the first time she'd laughed in days. "Charlotte, I have ammo. All I have to do is wave your fried chicken under any of the men's noses and they'll stop what they're doing and follow me. Then Steven will have to come, too, unless he wants to do all the work alone."

"You are a devil," Charlotte declared with a chuckle. "I can't think why I didn't like you that first day. You remind me of myself."

"Why, thank you, Charlotte. Now where's that basket? I am a woman on a mission. This little munchkin needs her daddy and I intend to rope him and bring him in, figuratively speaking of course."

Jackie started heading toward the door.

"Jackie?" Charlotte called.

Jackie turned.

"You might think about losing the pumps and the skirt if you're going to be walking around in the pastures. Wear boots and take my Jeep and the cell phone. Just in case you get lost or stuck or stepped on or mashed up," she added. "A horse would be better, but…"

"I know, I know. I'm a city girl, and I don't know how to ride a horse." Jackie sighed in frustration.

Charlotte looked apologetic. "Not exactly a crime."

Jackie gave her a you've-got-to-be-kidding look. "It's not a crime at La Torchére. Here, it turns me into an outsider."

"You don't have to go out there looking for him."

Jackie looked at Suzy. Even in sleep she didn't seem as happy as usual. "Yes, I do," she said. "This baby needs her father." She didn't want to think about the fact that her own heart was soaring at the thought of seeing Steven again. Steven didn't want a woman. She wondered if he was still in love with his wife. Not that it mattered. They had both agreed they wouldn't suit.

"Just get the boots," she told herself as she marched upstairs. "And try not to look too much like a city girl." And try even harder not to look too eager to throw yourself in Steven's arms.

* * *

"Damn it all, Ben," Steven said. "I can't believe I did that. It's been years since I've been young enough to have an excuse for driving a vehicle into a ditch." He looked at the truck sitting half in the mud.

Ben took his hat off and scrubbed one hand back through his thinning hair. "Could be your mind was about as far away as a teenage boy's. Could be you were thinking about something else...or someone else."

Steven didn't even try to pretend he didn't know what Ben was talking about. "No excuses. If I was thinking about someone else, then I shouldn't have been."

Ben didn't argue with him.

"Well, we'd better try to move this thing," Steven said. "Should I call Hoagie?"

"Nah, I gave him and Ed a truckload of work this morning. I'd rather not pull them in if I don't have to."

Ben grinned. "You mean you'd rather not let them see that the boss does stupid things, too, now and then?"

Steven laughed. "That's about it." But inside he wasn't laughing. He'd done more stupid things since Jackie had come into his life than he could remember doing in years. He wondered when he would get back to being sensible and content again. "Get in the cab, Ben. I'll push."

Ben did, but the truck was having none of it. The wheels spun in the mud.

Steven slammed his hat against the back of the truck. "All right, let's try again. Let's see if you can't back it up just a bit and we'll get a fresh start." And he moved out of the way.

"Need some help?" At the sound of Jackie's cheerful voice, both Steven and Ben stopped what they were doing and turned to look. She was leaning out the driver's side of Charlotte's flame-red Jeep. Her eyes were wide, as was her smile. She was just about the prettiest thing Steven had ever seen. He wanted to scoop her up and eat her right then and there, but at that moment Ben cleared his throat. He cleared it twice, ending on a sound that resembled a donkey's bray. Steven remembered that he was supposed to be staying away from Jackie.

"Where's Suzy?" he asked, forcing himself to make his voice deep and grumpy.

"Sleeping." Jackie didn't lose her smile. Damn the woman. Didn't she know that she was in danger of being kissed if she didn't stop looking at him that way?

Steven stared.

Ben cleared his throat more forcefully. He was practically coughing now.

"You really should do something about that throat, Ben," Jackie told him. "I probably have something back at the house that would help. If not, I'm sure Charlotte has some home remedy she could mix up. We'll do that, just as soon as we get your truck out of the mud. What can I do to help here?"

And just like that, she hopped out of the Jeep, an eager look on her face. She was wearing jeans that hugged her hips and a cute little formfitting T-shirt that had tumbling teddy bears on the front—probably something that Charlotte had picked up in town for her, since he had seen them at the local department store. She was half a foot shorter than either he or Ben and a good deal lighter. He remembered that she had been raised in the city.

Steven exchanged a look with Ben, then turned back toward Jackie. He couldn't help smiling at her. Heck, he couldn't seem to stop looking at Jackie, and he realized that it seemed like forever since he had last seen her. "You just stay right where you are," he said in a voice that seemed to catch. "Ben and I are used to this sort of thing, and if we can't get it out, we have men we can call on."

Jackie gave him a weary, patient look. "Do not patronize me, Rollins. I may have been born in the city, I may not know which end of a horse is the one you feed the carrots to, I may be skittish around cows and other barnyard animals, and I may even be smaller than you. But I learned how to drive anything on wheels when I was barely old enough to have a driver's license. My mother liked to be chauffeured, and she changed cars every few months." Her tempo had picked up as she talked. Her blue eyes were practically flashing sparks.

Steven grinned. "You're incredibly pretty when you get indignant," he said, wondering where those words had come from. Jackie stopped short.

"Are you trying to distract me, Steven Rollins?"

Distract her? A vision of himself reeling her in tight against his body, laying his lips on hers, sliding his palms over her breasts and doing his best to distract her, came to mind. It was all he could do to stand still and not grab for her.

"I'm just saying that this is a big truck," he said, totally changing the subject.

"And I may not be nearly as big as you or Ben, but I could at least drive while the two of you push. That wouldn't be so tough, would it? I promise not to run you down. Unless you start insulting me again."

Ben gave a choked laugh.

Steven gave her a slow smile. "Was I insulting you? When? When I said that you were pretty?"

"I don't like to be lied to or manipulated, and that's what you were trying to do. That's what was insulting. I'm not pretty and never have been," she said.

Steven shook his head. "Lady, you are so dead wrong it doesn't even bear speaking about. And I would never insult you. So get out of the truck, Ben, and let her in."

Ben gave him an incredulous look. "You're going to trust someone that little with a truck this size?"

"I trust her with my child," Steven said quietly.

And Ben shut up. Good thing, too, because within minutes—and with the two of them pushing—Jackie had guided the truck out of the ditch.

She climbed out of the truck and tossed Ben the keys. "Charlotte has fried chicken and peach pie at the house," she told him.

Ben stared at her. He looked away, then shook his head, hitting his hat against his leg.

"Fresh from the oven peach pie," Jackie whispered.

"Dammit, don't do that," Ben said. Then he turned to Steven. "What can I say? She knows my weakness, and I don't think you're going to want me here anyway. I'm headed for the house. Be careful." And he drove off and left Jackie alone with Steven.

After Ben's departure, all that could be heard was

the humming of insects and the songs of the birds. Jackie found a dry, green patch of ground and plopped herself down. "I brought the picnic basket, if you're hungry."

He sat beside her. "Fried chicken and peach pie? I'm not Ben. I'm not that easy. And, no, I'm not hungry yet. You wanted something, I figure. Let's get to it."

"How do you figure?"

He held out his big hands, palms out. "You've stayed near the house most of the time you've been here. I've never once seen you drive Charlotte's Jeep, and she doesn't loan it to just anyone, or for frivolous reasons."

Jackie nodded. "You're right. I have an agenda and it's not a frivolous one. I want you to come home."

Steven's breath froze in his chest. *Home,* she had said, but he knew she didn't mean it that way. He shook his head. "When I'm home, I…crowd you." He looked at her and let her see the naked, heated desire in his eyes. He did not want her misunderstanding him. He wanted to touch her very badly. He wanted her in his bed, every cell of her naked body against his. No space between them, no room for anything except raw passion.

The pulse at the base of her throat fluttered. "I crowd you, too," she said in a shaky voice, "but that can't matter right now. Suzy needs you. She misses you. That's not right."

Steven ran his hand over his face. He left it there for a second, not wanting to face his dilemma.

"Do you miss your wife?" Jackie asked suddenly. "Do I make it worse?"

He lowered his hand and looked into her eyes. "My

wife and I—our marriage wasn't idyllic. She wasn't happy here, or with me. When she met me, I was a rising college football star. I guess she thought that even though I busted up my knee, I would still be able to take her to high places. She never quite adjusted to married life. She especially hated being forced back to the ranch. By the time she died, we were reasonably content, but not in love. We settled for what we could manage. So, no, you don't make it worse, not in the way you mean."

She blinked. "Your staying away, the way things began with us...I thought...you didn't dislike me so much anymore."

She shifted, and heat flooded his body. "I don't dislike you. I like you too much. I can't be near you without wanting to touch you. So, yes, in that way, you make it worse, but that's not your fault. It's mine."

"I want to touch you, too."

"Aw, damn, don't say that. Don't let me know that. Because if I know that, I'll take advantage. I can't do that to you, because I can't make promises to any woman anymore. My career fell apart, my marriage fell apart. I don't want to chance anything else falling apart, ever again, especially not when Suzy will soon be old enough to be affected."

"I know, but I'm going soon. What could happen?"

He stared at her, incredulous. He reached out and ran the tip of one index finger gently down the side of her cheek. He traced a path along her jaw and down her throat. His finger dipped in the vee of her blouse, grazing her breast.

She flinched and sucked in a deep breath.

"What could happen?" he asked. "I'd say…a lot. A lot that neither of us wants, at least in the long term."

Slowly, shakily she nodded. Then she stared directly into his eyes. "I agree that there are risks, but I don't like what this is doing to Suzy, and I don't want my time here to end on a sad note. Nothing can happen if we don't let it. Let's not let anything happen. We can both be strong. I trust you."

Steven gave a low growl. "Well, that makes one of us. Come on, let's go back. I guess we can find some way to avoid being in the same place at the same time for too long."

Jackie studied him. "You're right. We need a plan. I'm good at those."

Steven grimaced. "I thought I had a plan. Ben was supposed to knock me down if I tried to get near you."

She laughed, a twinkle in her eyes. "I'm stronger than Ben."

Steven looked at her. "I'm beginning to think that you're stronger than most people I know. This plan you're working on, make it rock solid. You and I don't need any more unexpected babies."

She gave a tight nod. "We don't want any unexpected anything. I'll think of something to keep us apart."

Chapter Twelve

"There must be something wrong with either my eyesight or this mirror," Jackie whispered as she peered at herself. Her eyes looked brighter and her lips turned up more than they normally did, it seemed. Her entire face looked lit up somehow.

"Silly. Nothing wrong with the mirror. It's just the company you've been keeping." Steven and Suzy. Not that she saw Steven very much. She made a point of keeping her distance, because they both wanted it that way. But still, she could feel him in the house. She could tell that Suzy was happier. When she had read Suzy the story of *The Ugly Duckling* earlier that morning, Suzy had jabbered happily. She had kissed the picture book and beamed at Jackie. Those moments alone were enough for joy. Suzy's increased happiness was entirely due to her father's return into her life.

But trying to keep her own distance from Steven was so difficult, Jackie conceded. And now, she could hear him up and moving around the house.

"Time to take a walk for a while," she decided. And she pulled on her boots, grabbed her bag of knitting and headed for the door.

"Are you off again?" Charlotte asked.

"I'll be back soon. After breakfast, I promise. I'll help you with lunch."

Charlotte frowned. "I'm not complaining about the work. I'm complaining about the fact that you're skipping breakfast again."

Jackie wrinkled her nose and then smiled. "Am not." She grabbed a muffin off the plate that Charlotte was carrying and then started to scoot out the door.

"That's not breakfast—not a whole one, anyway," Charlotte grumbled. "Jackie."

"Yes, Jackie," a deep male voice said.

Jackie whirled to see Steven standing there. "Is this your great agenda?" he asked. "You starve and walk your legs off while I get to eat at my leisure?"

She crossed her arms. "Walking is very healthy."

"Not eating is not. Now come on in and eat breakfast with me."

"But you said…"

"I know what I said. I didn't think you were going to starve yourself to accommodate me. Don't worry, I'll put the whole length of that six-foot table between us, and I'll mind my manners. Charlotte will smack me if I don't, won't you, Charlotte?"

"You touch her, I'll wallop you with the frying pan," Charlotte said with a laugh.

Jackie could feel the heat climbing up her throat. "I hardly think that will be necessary."

"Honey," Charlotte said, one hand on her hip, "He's a man. Sometimes they just need smacking."

"You've smacked a lot of men?" Steven asked with a slow smile.

"I walloped Ned Battleman once. Course lately, I've been kind of partial to him. He called me last night. I might even let him kiss me one of these days."

Jackie's eyes widened. She looked at Steven, who was grinning. "Ned's one lucky man, Charlotte. Maybe I should be the one wielding the frying pan—to protect you from him."

"Hmpff. Maybe I don't want protecting," Charlotte declared. "Maybe Jackie doesn't either."

Jackie saw Steven's eyes turn dark and fierce. She thought that maybe Charlotte was right. But what she wanted didn't much matter, not when Suzy was at stake. She opened her mouth to protest.

"Oh, don't worry," Charlotte said. "I know you two have your own plans. Now go eat your breakfast."

So Jackie moved into the dining room. Steven stepped around her and pulled out her chair. She felt his body close behind hers as she sat. She worked hard to repress her need to touch him and have him touch her.

But then he was moving away and heading to the other end of the table. The room grew quiet, the clink of china and silver loud in the stillness. She couldn't help wondering what it must have been like when

Steven sat here with his wife. Had they talked about the baby on the way? He'd said they were content in the end. Did he miss that? This forced silence between them was so tense, so unnatural.

As if he'd heard her thoughts, he cleared his throat. "Is there anything I can do to make your last days here easier, happier?" he asked her.

He could throw caution to the wind. So could she, but that kind of thing always ended up with a price. She shook her head. "I've enjoyed these past few days. Suzy and I played. I read her stories. I walked. Your land is very beautiful. I'm even beginning to develop muscles." She looked down at where her legs rested beneath the table.

"I'm glad that you're happy, that this turned out all right for you," he said.

She wouldn't exactly say that. When she left Rollins Acres, she was going to leave a big piece of her heart here, and not just with Suzy. But that would be the stupidest thing to say.

"I have to go," she said. "I'm walking as much of Rollins Acres as I can. I have it all mapped out. If I leave now, I can cover a lot of ground today."

And she started to rise, to run from her thoughts. He stood when she did. "Jackie…" Steven began, just as the phone rang in the other room.

She couldn't stop, couldn't talk to him right now. If she did, she might tell him how she felt, that she didn't want her time with him to end just yet.

"Jackie, it's for you," Charlotte called.

Jackie rushed from the room. She took the call upstairs.

"Jackie, please, I know you've got a couple more

days, but everything is getting so complicated," Parris said. "All this paperwork, all these people demanding things. I think we're going to lose the Pollock. And Dad called last night. I think he might be waiting for the ax to fall. He didn't seem happy that I was having trouble with the auction or that you weren't here. You know what's going to happen if things fall through."

The old panic began to build inside her. "I know, Parris." But once she left Rollins Acres, she would never see Suzy or Steven again. That pain was knifelike. It stole her breath. It stole everything good inside her. She still had a little more time here. They might be tortuous days, spent wishing she could be with Steven and knowing that she couldn't, but they were all she had left. And when she left, she wanted her goodbyes to be leisurely and final and the best she could manage.

"Just hold on for a few more days, Parris. I promise I'll come right back and help you when this is over."

The silence on the other end of the line was thick. "Goodbye, Jackie," Parris finally said, and she hung up.

Jackie didn't feel good about that. She didn't feel good about anything. Rushing for the door, she grabbed up her bag of knitting and started walking. Maybe if she walked far enough and fast enough she could stay ahead of her fears and desires and the truth. In a couple of days, she would be back at La Torchére, and it would be as if she had never met Steven Rollins or his daughter.

Except in her heart, where the pain would never stop. Because her heart would stay here with the man and child she loved.

Her eyes began to mist. Jackie blinked hard to hold

her tears at bay. She sat down on a rock, pulled out her knitting and blindly plied the needles. For hours she sat there, trying to concentrate, working feverishly to finish, to tidy up the loose ends—not just of the blanket but of her heart.

It couldn't be done. Everything was a mess.

She rose from her perch and began walking. She looked off in the distance and saw that the clouds had formed into beautiful, puffy shapes against the clear blue of the sky.

Steven and Suzy saw this all the time, she thought, whereas she would never stand under this particular sky again. When she left, it would be as if she had never been here at all. Years would pass. Steven would forget her, and Suzy would never remember she existed. That was the way it should be. It was what she had told him she wanted when she came here.

So why were there tears spilling down her cheeks?

But Jackie didn't even bother trying to answer the question. The answer was so obvious.

"I love you, Steven Rollins," she whispered. "And Parris is right. It's time to go."

And that was when she stepped in the hole and fell. The earth came up to meet her, and the green grass turned black.

Someone was carrying her. No, not someone. Steven. Jackie knew the strength of those arms. She knew that masculine scent of bay rum, leather, horses and man. She just knew, because her heart was full.

She took a deep breath, her muscles tightening.

"Don't even think about moving," he said. "You might have hit your head."

She reached up and felt. "No bumps," she told him in a whisper. His arms tightened around her. She could stay right here forever.

And if she did…well, he didn't want that.

"I have to leave," she told him. "Right now. Today. I promised Parris." It was so easy to lie when the alternative was risking the contentment of someone you loved. He'd been telling her for days that she made him crazy, that he felt an urgent physical need for her. She wouldn't lie to herself and pretend that he wouldn't take care of that need once she had gone. Steven wasn't a man who could live his whole life like a monk. Once she was out of here, his world would settle down. He would be content again, as he had been with his wife.

"Steven, did you hear me? I have to leave."

He stopped walking. He looked down at her, his jaw tight, his eyes darker than usual. "The doctor's on his way to the house. I'm not sending you anywhere without his okay. All right?"

She nodded and felt slightly dizzy, but she was pretty sure the doctor would let her go.

"How did you step into that hole, anyway?"

She squirmed. "I was looking at the clouds."

He sighed.

"I know," she said. "In the city, that's fine. Out here, you have to pay more attention to where you step. You know me."

"City girl," he agreed, but it didn't sound like an insult. It sounded like resigned acceptance. She supposed he was right. A woman raised to a ranch wouldn't have twisted her ankle in a hole. But the thought of leaving gave her such a profound sense of sadness that it was difficult to think of herself as a city girl now.

Steven stopped for a moment. He gazed down at her. "If you go, if the doctor lets you leave now, I'll wait until everything clears up for you and your sister. Then I'll bring Suzy to the resort so you can have your last days with her. The bargain was for two weeks. I want you to have your two weeks."

But she wanted more than two weeks. She wanted forever. It was tearing her apart inside. If she said goodbye now, and then had to do it again…

"It's okay," she said, daring to touch his arm, allowing herself to feel the bittersweet joy of being connected to him. "You've met your end of the bargain, as far as I'm concerned. When I go, I want that to be it." Her voice was strong, or at least as strong as she could make it.

He studied her for a long while, his gaze taking in each detail of her countenance. His eyes looked like dark coals, so dark she couldn't read what he was feeling.

Finally he gave a tight nod and began walking again. Soon enough, Steven had her home. The doctor was waiting, and he pronounced her a little bruised but otherwise healthy. She should take it easy for the rest of the day, but essentially there was nothing keeping her from making her exit.

Except her heart, and her heart had wanted things it couldn't have before. She had learned not to pay attention to it. The fact that the pain was deeper and greater than she had ever known couldn't matter.

"I'll go pack," she told Steven.

He nodded. "I'll take you back."

The pain grew more intense. She could barely breathe. "Do you mind—would it be all right if Ben took me back?"

He looked as if she had hit him. She knew he was thinking that she didn't trust him. It wasn't that at all. She was just afraid that if she had to say goodbye to him when there were no others around, she might lose control. Then she might ask him for things he could never give, things like his love, his heart, a future with her. So she kept silent. She didn't correct him and tell him that she trusted him the way she'd trusted no other man in her lifetime.

"I'll get Ben," he told her.

"I'll pack and say goodbye to Charlotte and Suzy." Jackie barely got the words past the lump in her throat.

She went through the motions of packing her things like a mechanical doll. She moved into Suzy's room and nearly stumbled as the realization of all she was losing hit her.

Picking up the little girl, she pulled her close and buried her face in Suzy's soft skin. She fought the tears that threatened to start again and never stop.

Suzy cooed and patted Jackie. "Ja," she said in a soft, caressing voice.

And then the tears began again, a torrent that threatened to tear Jackie apart. She kissed the child that she had once helped to make, then gently placed her back in her playpen and all but ran from the room.

Steven was standing just outside the door.

Not thinking, unable to think, she threw herself into his arms and kissed him.

His arms tightened around her. He held her and stroked his palm down her back. When she started to pull away, he kissed her again—a kiss of searing heat, a kiss meant to last forever.

"I'll tell her about you. She won't forget," he said, his voice thick.

And then Jackie pulled back and stared up into his eyes, her own filled with tears, his dark and worried. "I won't forget, either," she said. "Not any of it. Not one minute, Steven. Do you understand?" Did he understand what he'd given her? The acceptance, the desire—it had all been so much more than she had ever expected. It had been everything that she ever wanted and never had.

"I'll remember," she whispered again.

"Remember this, then," he said and he kissed her once more, this time gently, lingeringly. And then he turned her over to Ben and she moved out to the truck.

As they sped away over the rough earth, Rollins Acres fell away behind them like a fairy tale fading into the mist of her memory. Everything was over. She would always be a city girl remembering her cowboy and her cowgirl child for the rest of her life.

"No, no, no, she can't be leaving," Merry cried. She gave Lissa a desperate look.

"It's over, Merry," Lissa said, her voice resigned and sad. "You'll have to start again with two new people."

"But they were happy together. And they were good with their little girl together, weren't they?"

"It doesn't matter, Merry." Lissa reached out to touch Merry, but held back.

"But it does. There's no hope for happiness for them this way. And I—"

"I know," Lissa said. Merry was running out of time, and that was too bad. For a moment there she had been completely concerned for someone other than herself.

Oh well, this experiment with Steven and Jackie hadn't worked and there was nothing to be done about it. One of the most important rules of the curse was that Merry couldn't impose her will on others, and Jackie and Steven had made their choice.

There was no point in spending any more time trying to throw them together.

Chapter Thirteen

In spite of Suzy and Charlotte's constant presence, the house seemed empty after Jackie had left, Steven thought as his boots echoed across the old wooden floors. He passed Charlotte who gave him an exasperated look.

"You could go get her. You could take Suzy to visit her."

"No, that wouldn't be right. We made a deal for two weeks, and the two weeks are up, or mostly up."

"She might not feel the same way you do about deals."

Steven considered that, then dismissed it as wishful thinking, a dream. Dreams had never been his strong suit. Sitting tight, moving through life a day at a time without wishing for the impossible was his way. It had brought him Suzy and a modicum of contentment. Shooting for a dream might risk not only his own happiness but his child's.

"Suzy and I are fine," he said. And yet, ten minutes later, he found himself standing outside the door to Jackie's room, then stepping inside.

There was still a faint trace of her lily of the valley scent. He breathed it in. His knees nearly buckled, but he forced himself to stand up straight and keep moving.

There, on top of the dresser, was the bag that Jackie had used for her knitting. As if he couldn't stop himself, he reached inside and pulled out the finished soft yellow blanket. It was still crooked, still a bit lumpy in places, still a sad little thing, but he looked at every stitch and knew that each one of them had been knit with love. And knowing that, he knew that he had never seen any blanket more beautiful. Picking it up, he ran his fingers over the edges and thought of how much work and determination Jackie had put into this gift for her child.

His chest felt tight, his vision, blurred. He started to replace the blanket and realized that there was something else in the bag. Reaching in, he pulled out a note pinned to a navy blue scarf. *For Steven,* it read. *Thank you for sharing.*

As if he'd done something nice for her, as if he hadn't been a beast at the beginning.

"A scarf," he said, his voice thick. "Silly city girl. This is Florida. When would I ever wear a knitted scarf?"

But holding the soft yarn, remembering the pretty blue eyes of the woman who had labored over it, he could think of times when he would wear a scarf like this one. He might like to take Jackie to Vermont for Christmas. He might like to see her against the snow-topped trees, to make her laugh with a snowball fight, to lie with her in front of a fire. He could imagine holding her all night long as the snow shrouded the world around them...

He could dream of such things.

Steven took a deep breath. "Foolish, unrealistic, not possible," he said to himself. "Hell, I've got work to do. That's reality. That's what I need to concentrate on." And he put the blanket and scarf back where he had found them and left the room.

Jackie had been back at the resort for several days. Things should have started to return to normal, she thought as she went about getting ready for work. But despite the fact that she had managed to talk the donor of the Pollock out of taking it back, and the fact that she was making some progress with the auction, nothing felt right at all.

"Whew! Thank goodness you're back," Parris had told her when she had arrived, but Jackie couldn't seem to dredge up any enthusiasm for returning to the place where she belonged. What's more, she couldn't explain to Parris why she was so quiet and pale. She and Parris didn't talk about their feelings. They barely managed to talk at all most days.

"Are you feeling all right, Jackie? You look tired today," Ruthie Fernandez said, a worried look in her green eyes. Ruthie worked odd jobs at the resort. She and Jackie had come in contact often, and they had developed a friendship of sorts. Jackie had often noticed that Ruthie had sad eyes and that she never talked about her background—which suited Jackie just fine, since she didn't like to talk about herself, either. Ruthie had just brought Jackie some tea.

"Thank you, yes, Ruthie, I'm fine," Jackie began automatically, but then stopped and closed her eyes. "No, as a matter of fact, I'm not fine at all," she whispered. "I've done the most awful thing." The words slipped out as if she couldn't stop them.

For a minute Ruthie's eyes widened, no doubt because this personal comment was so unlike Jackie. But then the young woman recovered. She shook her head, her blond hair moving with her. "I don't believe it. We've talked often enough that I know you're not even capable of *awful*."

"But I am. These past couple of weeks, I've been off…"

"Visiting your daughter."

Jackie couldn't answer at first. The word *daughter* hung in the air. Finally, she shook her head. "I donated the eggs that helped create Suzy, but she was never mine. When her father came here to tell me about her, to ask me to sign papers relinquishing her, I…I blackmailed him into letting me see her and spend time with her."

Ruthie's brows raised, but she didn't look shocked. "Any mother would do the same, Jackie," she said gently.

"And then I fell in love with him when he had told me he didn't want to get involved ever again," Jackie said on a groan.

Ruthie moved closer and touched her friend's hair. "And your cowboy—does he love you, too?"

"I just told you—"

Ruthie shook her head and shushed Jackie. "You told me what he said. I want to know what he feels."

Jackie bit her lip. "He feels...desire. He doesn't feel love. And I...I'm afraid."

"Because you feel both?"

"Yes, and because I feel as if I've found something I've been searching for all my life, but it's unattainable."

Ruthie tutted and plumped a pillow on the bed. "You should tell him how you feel. You should go see him and the little one again. I don't like seeing you so sad."

Instantly, Jackie felt contrite. She touched Ruthie's hand. "I can't go see him. The truth is that I should never have insisted on seeing Suzy in the first place. I had no real right to her, and I had no right to burden you with my troubles. Friends don't do that."

Ruthie gave Jackie a small smile. "Friends share," she said, but Jackie noticed that Ruthie's eyes were sadder than usual and that she didn't offer to share any of her own troubles.

"I should just stick to work," Jackie said to herself after Ruthie had gone. "I should try to forget about Steven and Suzy and I definitely shouldn't discuss them with anyone else."

So when Merry came along later, Jackie was prepared to be as brief as possible, to make it clear that this wasn't a matter that was open to in-depth discussion. Merry had been asking pointed questions for days, and Jackie had taken to ducking down hallways when she saw her coming. No more.

"How is that handsome cowboy you were visiting?" Merry asked. "You haven't told me anything about your trip. Have you spoken with him?"

Jackie looked down at the papers on her desk. "I'm

afraid I've been very busy. I haven't had much time for conversations since I've been back, Merry."

"And how about that little girl? You did say he had a little girl, didn't you?"

Sighing, Jackie looked up. "He has a daughter, yes. Why?"

"Just wondering. Women adore men with children. I'll bet he has plenty of women fighting for his attentions, don't you think?"

"I wouldn't know." Which was a lie. She remembered the playgroup incident all too well.

"Well," Merry said, shrugging, "now that he's seen La Torchére, maybe someday he'll come back here on his honeymoon. This is a wonderful atmosphere for romance."

Jackie clutched her pen hard—so hard, it was a miracle the darn thing didn't break. Breathe in, breathe out, she ordered herself. Don't show any emotion. Talk. Answer the woman. Satisfy her curiosity so she'll move on to another topic. But, "La Torchére is a wonderful place," was all she could manage to say.

"Jackie?" Merry said, and the smile slid from her face. She looked worried. "You *are* all right, aren't you? I haven't gotten the chance to really talk to you since you've been back, and I really didn't mean to make you sad."

Jackie managed a tight nod. "I'm fine, Merry. Thank you." But the words came out on a whisper, and she couldn't quite manage to smile.

Merry's eyes filled with concern. She opened her mouth to speak, closed it again, then finally shook her head. "I'll check in with you later," she promised, twisting her hands together as she left the room.

"Later," Jackie agreed, but she didn't want to think about later. When the work day ended and she had no paperwork to distract herself with, thoughts of Suzy and Steven drifted in. And later, when she went to sleep, she couldn't hold her dreams of Steven at bay. Dreams so wonderful, she woke up feeling empty, because dreams were the only way she could ever see him again.

"You just have to forget him," she told herself. "Take it one day at a time, one night at a time. Eventually, you'll be able to make it through a whole night without thinking of him even once."

That had to be her mantra from now on.

There was no question, Merry thought, feeling a bit sick about her conversation with Jackie, but she had wanted to be sure. Now she was. Jackie was in love with Steven Rollins.

And Steven was miles away. Maybe he didn't feel the same way that Jackie did. To try to bring him here under such circumstances would be cruel to Jackie and probably to Steven, too. After the horse incident, she didn't want to risk hurting anyone. But she just couldn't let this drop.

Whipping out her cell phone, she stared at the screen until Rollins Acres appeared. Steven was on his horse out on the range, alone, doing his job, apparently just fine.

Then he turned, and she got a better view of him. He looked haggard, his normally broad shoulders drooped, his dark eyes were empty. No, not empty. Filled with despair.

"Please let it be love for Jackie," Merry whispered to herself as she flipped the phone closed. "Please don't let me make a mistake and hurt someone."

She disappeared into her office, telling her secretary that she was not to be disturbed. She needed to think this one out and come up with a plan.

Somehow she had to get them together in the same room. But, so far, all of her plans had gone awry, and she was feeling a little desperate…

"What do you mean, Suzy is sick?" Jackie felt her throat closing up, her heart beginning to pound like a heavy, relentless sledgehammer.

Merry shook her head. "I—I don't know." Her voice was tight, slightly uncertain. She wouldn't quite look at Jackie. "I took the call. For some reason, I couldn't get through to you. Your cowboy, Steven, said that it was urgent. He said that she was sick and that he wanted you to know…"

Merry's voice faded away, but it didn't matter. Jackie was already running from the conference room where Merry had found her. She headed for the nearest phone, her heart thudding in her ears. Suzy, her little girl. So ill that Steven had called to tell her about it? Jackie couldn't bear to think of how serious the situation must be.

She didn't even have to look up the number. She had almost called Steven in a weak moment yesterday, before reason had taken hold.

"Please be there," she whispered. "Please pick up."

Charlotte answered. Charlotte would know about Suzy. But Charlotte hadn't called Merry, and even if she had…

"Charlotte, is Steven there? This is Jackie. I need to talk to him if he is. Please."

"Jackie? Jackie?"

"Yes." She could barely get that one word out. Fear and nerves made her voice weak and small.

Fortunately, Charlotte was a smart woman. "Hold on," she said. "He's right here."

Jackie heard muffled whispering in the background. Charlotte must have placed her hand over the receiver.

"Jackie?" Steven's deep voice came over the line. Nothing had ever sounded so good. Except she couldn't feel good because Suzy…

"How is she?" Jackie asked suddenly. "Is she going to be all right?"

"Who? Jackie, darlin'…"

The unexpected endearment caught Jackie by surprise and right in the heart. For a moment she couldn't breathe. She almost couldn't think straight. "Merry said that you told her that Suzy was really sick. I called right away. I was so worried, so scared. She's so little and helpless. Steven, how bad is she? And how are you handling all this? I wish I were there helping you right now."

"Sick? Suzy? Jackie, hon," he said, his voice low and deep and soothing, "Suzy's just fine. There's not a thing wrong with her. I don't know why Merry would say that. I haven't even spoken to her since that day I picked you up at the resort."

"You haven't?" Confusion flooded Jackie's mind and then deep, dark embarrassment flowed in. Steven probably thought she was just playing some kind of dumb game. Like those women at the playgroup.

"I'm…forgive me for calling. I'm so sorry," she began. "I don't know why Merry told me that, but

I…well, I feel like a complete idiot. Please, just forget I even called. Goodbye, Steven."

She rushed to hang up the phone. For a second, she thought she heard Steven yell "Wait!" but then she placed the receiver back in the cradle and moved away as if the phone were on fire.

She covered her face with her hands. "What was that about?" she whispered. "What must he think of me now?"

And then she allowed herself to remember how it had felt to hear his voice. For five seconds she closed her eyes and concentrated on Steven's voice and what it did to her. It filled her soul, made her whole, even if just for a short time.

What had Merry been doing? Jackie shook her head. She regretted looking like an idiot, but she didn't regret having had the chance to hear his voice one more time. Maybe she should thank Merry for her lie.

"Oh, what a pathetic creature you are, Jackie Hammond," she whispered. "Mooning after a man's voice on the telephone, even when you called him for a made-up reason." She moaned in frustration and hugged her arms tightly around her body. How long was she going to be this way, and when was she going to start getting better? And what was it that Merry had been trying to do?

She had a terrible feeling that she knew. She just hoped that Steven didn't suspect there had been matchmaking going on.

Steven stood staring at the receiver as the silent phone mocked him. She was gone. Here unexpectedly and then just…gone. And he felt as though he wanted to crawl right through the telephone lines to get to her.

He felt as though life was going to lose its meaning if he didn't at least hear her, see her, taste her one more time.

"Why did she think Suzy was sick?" Charlotte asked, frowning in confusion.

"I don't know. Something Merry, the resort manager, told her. I don't get it."

But Charlotte was looking speculative.

"What?"

"Did you meet this Merry?"

"Sure. She took me to Jackie when I met her at the resort. Set us up in some secluded little place on the beach surrounded by palm trees." And with a double hammock, he remembered, swallowing hard, wishing he had Jackie and that double hammock close at hand right now.

"Merry took you somewhere so you could be alone with Jackie?"

"Yes, we were going to talk business."

"Business? In a secluded place on the beach?" Charlotte sounded skeptical.

"Yeah, it was kind of unusual, but nice," he said, and he remembered Jackie's pretty blue eyes. What he wouldn't give to have one more chance to talk business with her. Or talk about anything with her.

"And now she's back at the resort," Charlotte said, "worried sick about that baby. And that baby is…"

"Fretful," Charlotte and Steven both said at once, and Charlotte smiled. "And you're—"

"Miserable," Steven said.

"That Merry, what a liar," Charlotte said, but she didn't sound upset.

"Terrible woman," Steven agreed. "I think I might have to go to La Torchére and give her a piece of my mind. Pack some clothes for yourself and Suzy, Charlotte. I might need your help."

"Telling Merry off?"

"Not exactly." But he didn't elaborate further, and Charlotte didn't ask.

Steven paced inside the bower, as much as it was possible to pace inside a space that small. He tugged at his red silk tie and tried not to be nervous. What in heck was taking the woman so long, anyway?

Then he heard voices. "Merry, from now on if there are customers to see me, I'd just as soon meet them in my office."

"You don't like our bowers?"

"I do. They're beautiful. It's just that they're a little…"

Jackie's voice was so close. Steven leaned outside the bower, took her hand and pulled her inside with him. She gasped and he smiled down into her eyes. "They're a little too romantic for business," he said, continuing to gaze into those pretty blue eyes.

"Steven!"

"None other."

She shook her head. "I don't understand. I—" And then those blue eyes filled with concern. "There *is* something wrong with Suzy, isn't there? You just didn't want to scare me by telling me over the telephone."

He shook his head, mentally kicking himself for scaring her. "There's nothing wrong with Suzy, not in the way you mean. She's completely healthy, but she does miss you."

Jackie closed her eyes. "You're just saying that."

"No." He took a step closer. He thought her breath hitched up a bit, but then maybe that was just wishful thinking. "She hugs her teddy bears tighter these days. That's a sure sign that something's not completely right. And my stories aren't nearly as good as yours are. She needs you, Jackie. She needs...her mother."

He was hoping to make her smile, but instead her eyes filled with tears that broke his heart to bits.

"Don't," he said. "Please. I'm not lying, Jackie. I came partly to let you know that I've torn up that paper that you signed. I'm not going to ask you to give up your rights to Suzy. It's a done deal. Suzy is your child, too, and I want my daughter to have you in her life, a woman who loves her and will always be there for her." He stroked his palm down her cheek.

"She has Charlotte."

"She needs both of you."

"Steven," Jackie said on a choked whisper, "you are such a good man, such a good father."

"No." He shook his head. "Because if I were a good man, I wouldn't have told you that before I told you what I really came here for."

Jackie tilted her head, confusion in her eyes.

He held up one hand. "I just want you to know that no matter what, Suzy remains your daughter. Michelle carried her and she'll always be a part of Suzy, but you gave her life, you loved her. I won't ever interfere with that or seek to bar you from her."

"Steven, are you very sure?" Her voice trembled. She clutched the back of a chair.

"I've never been more sure of anything."

"And I've never been given a greater gift. I promise you that I will treasure every moment you ever allow me with her, and I'll never do anything that could possibly hurt her."

"That was never a question. I trust you with her the same way I trust myself." His voice dropped low. He stepped closer. "But none of that is why I came here today. I could have had a lawyer tell you all of that. I could have called. What I came for couldn't be left to a lawyer or taken care of over the phone."

"So...why did you come??" Her voice was soft and uncertain.

"I came to ask you a question." He hesitated, then reached out and gently grasped her chin. "I want you staring straight into my eyes when I ask you this. I need to see your reaction."

"Ask me anything," she whispered, staring straight into his eyes.

He nodded slightly. "I want to know...I need to know if it's possible that you could ever come to care for a man who runs a ranch."

Jackie closed her eyes. Steven nearly panicked. He flinched, his fingers tightened, but he immediately recovered, afraid he might have bruised her.

"Jackie?" His voice was hoarse.

She opened her eyes, and he saw that they were damp

but clear. She focused on him completely. "That man…he has to know that I'm not much of a rancher."

He swallowed. "Do you hate ranching so much?" He felt the seconds ticking by as he waited.

She shook her head, her soft skin sliding beneath his fingers. "No, I don't hate ranching. I love it, actually. When I was at Rollins Acres with you and Suzy, for the first time in my life, I felt like I belonged, that I was right where I wanted and needed to be, the place that I was born for. But…I know that I wasn't very helpful. Not the way a woman raised on a ranch would be."

"City girl," he said softly. "You helped me more than anyone had in years. You gave me what I needed. You filled my empty spaces, you made me want to dream again, but…"

"But what?" she asked, her voice breaking.

"But you still haven't told me if you could love a rancher. Not that I want you to worry about that. You don't have to love me. It's not a requirement."

And suddenly Jackie was pressing closer to him. She lifted her face, twined her arms around his neck and kissed him. Then she pulled back, her expression confused. "You wonderful rancher, you. How could I not love you? And how could you love a woman who has to take a deep breath every time she's near a horse?"

Steven chuckled. "It's impossible not to love you, and I ought to know. I tried my best not to fall in love with you, but you've got a heart as big as my ranch. You've got *my* heart. As for the horses, you'll lose your fear of them with time, or you won't. And if you don't, it won't be an issue, because you'll never lose my love. You'll always have me and our child."

"Our child. Thank you so much for that," she said.

"I didn't do anything. She was yours from the minute you smiled at her, and she's here for you right now. Charlotte has her, and I'll take you to see both of them in a few minutes. But first I have something I need to do."

And he pulled her close, wrapped his arms around her and kissed her the way he had been longing to for weeks, with passion and heat and love. It was a long kiss. When he raised his head, her lips were rosy and her eyes were dazed.

"Whew! Do all ranch boys learn to kiss like that?" she asked, her voice a little broken.

He smiled. "I hope this ranch boy is the only one you ever kiss. And no, I learned a lot on the ranch, but that was pure…you. I get a little crazy whenever you're near."

"Good. I've always been the sensible one, but I get a little crazy whenever I'm near you, too. And you know all those days I was walking around the ranch?"

"I was miserable every minute without you."

Jackie smiled. "I was, too, and I found a lot of places where a man and a woman can be alone and go crazy."

"Then I can't wait to get back to our ranch and visit every one of them with you, love."

She blinked. "Our ranch?"

He hesitated. "I guess I forgot to ask. Will you marry me, Jackie, love?"

"Yes, oh very much yes," she whispered. "And I'll love you and our daughter forever. I can't wait to get home to the ranch and begin."

Steven gave a whoop, and picked her up and swung her around. "Thank goodness for Merry and whatever her plan was. It made me realize how much I was missing. Now come closer, my pretty city girl."

He wrapped one hand around her waist and drew her closer.

"Let me kiss you again, my love," he whispered.

She moved back into his arms. "City or ranch, anytime, anywhere," she said. "I'm yours."

"Then right here, right now," he told her. And then he stopped talking and simply kissed the woman he loved with his whole heart.

Epilogue

"**I**'m worried," Merry said the next day.

"About what?" Lissa asked.

Merry shrugged. "About whether this match is going to be added to my total. Just about everything I tried ended up going wrong."

"Yes," Lissa said softly, "but when it really counted, things went right. Steven and Jackie are together, they're happy, and I think you might even be a bit elated about that fact yourself. Admit it. Here they come."

Merry watched as Jackie and Steven walked along the beach barefoot, Suzy on Steven's hip.

"They do look happy, don't they?" Merry asked, her gaze following them. "Not that it matters to me. I'm just glad I'm getting the credit and that I'm one step closer to my goal." But she didn't look away from the couple. Lissa thought she might have even heard a sigh.

At that moment, Jackie turned and waved. "Thank you, Merry," she called, just as Parris and Ruthie came around the corner and stopped beside Lissa.

Merry blinked. Then she waved back, and the four women began to talk.

"Why do you think she was matchmaking?" Jackie asked Steven.

"She probably wanted you to be happy."

Jackie smiled up at him. "I don't think you can ever know how truly happy you've made me. It's almost as if there's something magical in the air today."

Steven chuckled. "So you believe in magic?"

She bopped his arm lightly. "Are you making fun of me? Are you saying you're a skeptic?"

Stopping in his tracks, Steven gazed down at her. "No," he finally said, dropping a light kiss on her lips, then placing his arm around her as they continued to walk. "I had lost my belief in magic years ago, but now I know it's real. You've made it real for me."

"And you've done the same for me," she agreed, her voice low and dreamy. "You've made my dreams come true, and isn't that how every good fairy tale ends?"

"Not completely."

"No?" She sounded incredulous.

"No, I think a good fairy tale ends up with a lot of kissing and with a man and woman heading off to spend the day together. More practical, and very much what I'd like to do with you." He grinned at her. "See what you do to me? I can't stop thinking about touching you."

Jackie leaned against his arm and shook her head. "That…amazes me. It humbles me—especially since I ache to touch you, too. You know, I used to feel like an ugly duckling."

"You?" Steven asked. "Can't believe that. You are a swan, darlin'. An extremely lovely swan."

"I'm a swan who found my mate. I've found a man and a child who I love beyond belief."

"When we marry, will you want more children?" he asked. He stopped and faced her, waiting for her to speak.

She tilted her head up and gazed directly into his eyes. "Yes, I definitely want more children, if that's all right with you. Only, this time, I want to conceive them in the usual way."

"That sounds wonderful," Steven said, bending to whisper near her ear. "Can we discuss this further in private? I think our sweet little daughter might be getting sleepy, anyway."

Jackie leaned back against him. "She looks pretty bright-eyed to me, but I guess we can't be selfish. Other people want to meet her, I think." She took Suzy from him and gave her child a hug and a kiss. "Come on, sweetheart. I know a whole group of ladies who are just dying to spend some time with you."

"Ja?" Suzy asked.

"Oh yes, angel," Jackie said, nuzzling her daughter. "You're very popular, you know. I want to introduce you to some very special ladies I know. You entertain them for a bit, okay, love? Your daddy and I have something we need to talk about."

Jackie and Steven turned and walked toward the group of women.

"Merry, would you mind watching Suzy for us for a few minutes? Charlotte is taking a bubble bath right now." And Jackie held Suzy out to the older woman.

"I—well, I—" Merry's eyes widened, but she held out her hands and awkwardly took Suzy. Ruthie and Parris and Lissa gathered closer to gaze at the adorable little baby.

Jackie looked at her half sister, who studied her for long seconds, then nodded and turned back to the child. The two of them had been the only children their father had ever had. Suzy was the first new connection, another girl. Maybe someday they would talk about that.

"Don't worry, we'll all help," Ruthie assured Jackie. "We'll protect little Suzy as if she's made of gold."

"That's right," Merry said with a shooing motion. "You two, go, enjoy yourselves. Go…plan something."

"Thank you, ladies," Steven said with a slight, gentlemanly nod.

And then he turned to Jackie. "Come on, love, it's time."

"Time?" she asked with a smile as she took the hand he held out.

"Yes, time to plan our happily-ever-after."

And Jackie moved into his arms and kissed him. "I'm pretty fond of happily-ever-afters," she told him. "My favorite kind of ending."

"So let's begin the story," he agreed. "It all started

with this beautiful, golden-hearted woman and a hard-headed rancher."

She laughed. "Have I mentioned that I also love hard-headed ranchers?"

"I love you, city girl." And then he took her in his arms as the rest of the story began to unfold...

* * * * *

Don't miss the continuation of
In a Fairy Tale World...
Six reluctant couples. Five classic love stories. One matchmaking princess.
And time is running out!

RICH MAN, POOR BRIDE
by Linda Goodnight
Silhouette Romance #1742
Available November 2004

HER FROG PRINCE
by Shirley Jump
Silhouette Romance #1746
Available December 2004

ENGAGED TO THE SHEIK
by Sue Swift
Silhouette Romance #1750
Available January 2005

NIGHTTIME SWEETHEARTS
by Cara Colter
Silhouette Romance #1754
Available February 2005

TWICE A PRINCESS
by Susan Meier
Silhouette Romance #1758
Available March 2005

If you enjoyed what you just read,
then we've got an offer you can't resist!

Take 2 bestselling love stories FREE!

Plus get a FREE surprise gift!

SILHOUETTE Romance

COMING NEXT MONTH

#1742 RICH MAN, POOR BRIDE—Linda Goodnight
In a Fairy Tale World...
Ruthie Ellsworthy Fernandez is determined to steer clear of gorgeous military physician Diego Vargas and his wandering ways. Ruthie wants roots, a home and a family more than anything, and though Diego's promises are tempting, they're only temporary—aren't they?

#1743 DADDY IN THE MAKING—Sharon De Vita
Danger is Michael Gallagher's middle name. But when he comes to a rural Wisconsin inn to unwind and lay low, beautiful innkeeper Angela DiRosa and her adorable daughter charm their way into his life. And soon Michael is finding that risking his heart is the most dangerous adventure of all.

#1744 THE BOWEN BRIDE—Nicole Burnham
Can a wedding dress made from magical fabric guarantee a lasting marriage? That's what Katie Schmidt wonders about her grandmother's special thread. And when handsome single father Jared Porter walks into Katie's bridal shop, she wonders if the magic is strong enough to weave this wonderful man into her life for good.

#1745 A WHIRLWIND...MAKEOVER—Nancy Lavo
Maddie Sinclair is a walking disaster! But when she needs a date to her high school reunion, her friend Dan Willis uses his photographer's eye to transform her from mousy to magnificent. With her new looks, Maddie's turning heads...especially Dan's.

SRCNM1004